LET WILD WAVES ROAR

.

Birte Hosken

DEDICATION

I dedicate this book to my future son-in-law Luke Hall who encouraged me to self-publish and who helped me to with the technical aspects of producing this book.

Birte Hosken
2019

"Dad, the postman is here," Jordan shouts and with that he storms up the drive to greet him. I am in the back garden preparing a barbeque. I have had my 40th birthday the previous Saturday but due to work commitments I have not been able to celebrate with my friends. Angie, my wife, is inside getting changed so I have no option but to leave the sizzling sausages behind and chase after my eight-year-old son.

A little surprised that the postman has refused to hand Jordan the mail I wipe my greasy fingers in Angie's flowery apron. "I will need a signature, please," the postman explains, handing me a pen. Well aware of the hungry gazes from seagulls sitting on the roof tops of neighbouring properties, keenly observing my tasty sausages and ready to steal them off the grill, I scribble my name on the postman's small card. "Thank you and have a nice day," he says before walking off towards the house next door. Jordan has obviously lost interest. He decides to join his young sister and his mother indoors.

Pushing the letter I have just signed for into the back pocket of my well-worn jeans I return to the barbeque as fast as I can. It is a gorgeous summer's day but I don't really feel like celebrating. Angie and I have had problems lately. In fact our marriage has been rocky before our daughter was born and it has not been great since...

No good thinking about that now. I am running late and my guests will soon be arriving. As most of my friends' children are still young we are having a lunch time barbeque so that everyone can bring their kids.

I have barely turned my sausages over when Justin and Judy join me in the garden. Once you get to my age you don't have "best friends" anymore but I think I would describe Justin as my best mate. We are about the same age, he is a fellow car salesman, we play golf together and we generally get on really well. Justin is not married. He's been through a couple of relationships since I've known him but his latest girlfriend, Judy, is lovely. She's very pretty and she has a little boy from a previous relationship who has made friends with Jordan. Angie says that Justin is very good-looking but a bit shy. I have to admit he can be irritatingly awkward at times. Smiling and remembering that I have been quite rude to him on several occasions I now watch him carry a large crate of beer. Judy is holding her son Tom's hand. She is beautifully dressed as usual and smiling back at me. "Happy Birthday, Robby" she says then, quickly approaching the barbeque and planting a big kiss onto my sweaty cheek.

Just a few seconds later Charles and Barbara enter the premises. Barbara is Angie's best friend – and I mean best friend. Those two can be on the phone for hours. Goodness knows what they can talk about for such a long time but they do. Apart from being such a close friend she is Jordan's god-mother. Her husband Charles sells double-glazing, conservatories, garage doors – the lot. He is a lively chap but he usually drives me crazy after about half an hour when he tries to get me to make home improvements for the umpteenth time. I very much hope he is going to resist it today. The couple have two girls, Samantha who is twelve and Suzanne who is ten.

I am glad that Angie is finally ready and greeting the guests. Our little girl, Melanie, has just learned to walk. Strangely enough she is quickly making a bee line for Justin. Everyone is laughing as she clings on to his legs for dear life.

My other guests are John and Anne, our neighbours on the left with their children Holly and Jacob and James-Peter, commonly known as JP, and his wife Freya from next door on the right. Their children have grown up but Freya does a spot of baby-sitting for us and with JP being a doctor we often call on them for help.

I have also invited my colleague Jackie but she generally declines when it comes to social events with partners. I have this odd feeling that she prefers women to men and she finds being among all these straight happy couples a little difficult.

Tom, Jordan and Jacob have started to knock a football around the garden but the girls are looking distinctly bored. Justin has not been able to move an inch since Melanie has got hold of him. Luckily Angie has supplied him with a drink so he doesn't have to suffer too much.

It is extremely hot doing the barbeque. The sweat keeps pouring off me. "Would you like me to take over for a while, Rob? You haven't had a chance to open your presents yet," JP offers kindly. Taking a large sip of beer I smile gratefully. "Yes, that would be great," I reply, ready to dress the medic up in Angie's colourful, and by now pretty grubby, apron. As I leave the doctor in charge of my grill I spot Justin joining in with the football. He has managed to hand Melanie over to Judy who seems popular with the young girls. They are helping her decorate my cake with 40 small candles.

After a couple of drinks in the searing sunshine I am starting to relax. I am really enjoying myself until the beer is beginning to go through me and I make my way indoors. It's a good job the neighbours on both sides have been invited as the noise in the garden is quite incredible. I can hear Angie tell Jordan off. Seems like he has kicked Tom in the shin and he is not prepared to apologise. Feeling a little light-headed I arrive at the bathroom. Tonight, when everyone has gone home, I must confess to Angie that I have applied for a job just over the border in Devon. I know she won't like it but I don't want her to find a letter from the dealership in Plymouth… - oh, dear, I have almost forgotten about today's mail. There is a letter in my back pocket that even I have not looked at yet.

Taking a deep breath I lock myself into our bathroom and pull the letter out of my jeans. The once pristine envelope looks all creased up now. Curiously I inspect the postmark. This is not what I am expecting. It is a letter from a firm of solicitors. Urgently I lean over to where my toothbrush is stored and use it as a letter opener. "Dear Mr Cunningham…" I read, and the more I read the more the letters are dancing in front of my eyes. Shaking my head I put the toilet seat down so I can sit down reasonably comfortably. Gasping I get up again to splash my face with cold water. This is a total surprise. It appears that I have inherited a cottage, a cottage in a village near Newquay. I still can't believe what I am reading. Looking at my watch I realise that it is time for me to return to my party. I don't want anyone worrying about my whereabouts. Sighing I quickly put the letter back into the half-torn envelope and stuff it back into my pocket.

From the moment I've left the bathroom my mind is on nothing but this letter. My confusion must be written all over my face. "You look a bit pale, Robby. Are you feeling OK?" Barbara asks me as I return to the garden. Putting on a broad smile I nod confidently but deep inside I am a worried man. The prospect of having to talk to Angie about my application, and then this unexpected inheritance – perhaps I should leave telling her about that until I have actually seen the cottage....

The consumption of so much alcohol in the lunch time heat has not done me any good at all. Instead of playing the happy birthday boy I feel rather grumpy. It is not until we all sit down around the table and Charles is starting on his double-glazing business that I completely lose the plot. "Listen, I have other things to worry about than your overpriced bloody plastic frames!" I shout at him. Barbara and Angie look at each other indignantly. Judy is smiling shyly at Justin who I know will be cringing deep inside. John and Anne appear not to have heard me but JP and Freya look visibly shocked by my outburst. The kids, both boys and girls, are finally amusing themselves but it has gone embarrassingly quiet at the table. "Well, perhaps it is best if we make a move now," Charles announces, his light blue eyes directed to his wife. He is getting up from his chair but Barbara is reluctant. "I am sure Rob didn't really mean what he just said," Angie says, trying to rescue the situation. She looks at me, pleadingly. *"Please apologise to him, please!"* her eyes are saying but I remain motionless. Barbara feels more than uncomfortable and calls for her children. "We are off home," she tells them. There is just a little bit of protest from the youngsters but minutes later they are ready to leave. I am glad that Melanie needs a nappy change so I make my excuses and take her inside.

I know Angie is furious. How dare I upset her best friend's husband – and not even apologise for my behaviour? She has gone up the drive with Barbara and Charles to see them off. It is Judy who suggests that Justin should go and find out what is wrong with me. I know this because he tells me so when he catches up with me in Melanie's room. Watching me clean up my little daughter he smiles. "You were out of order, Rob but I do sympathise. I've had to listen to that guy earlier and when I told him that I've just bought a new house, all double-glazed, he still wouldn't stop," he says to make me feel better about myself. "I could do with another cold beer," I simply reply kissing my daughter's tiny forehead. "Ok, I'll organise a couple of drinks for us," Justin volunteers and leaves us alone for a while. I pick Melanie up and carry her downstairs.

John and Anne are ready to go home as well, by far too early for Angie's liking. Her angry gaze meets me at the bottom of the staircase. "Why does Jacob have to go now? We've only just started another game," Jordan complains to his mother. She does not respond. Then Tom follows his friend, football in hand. "Are you going to play with us, Rob?" he asks me. I am shaking my head, feeling like a proper spoil-sport. "I am just going to have a drink with

Justin. I'll play a bit later maybe," I say rather awkwardly. Both Tom and Jordan look miffed. Angie takes over, pushing the two boys back into the garden and taking Melanie off my hands without a further word.

Heaving a temporary sigh of relief I wait for Justin to return with the beer. Impatiently I shift up and down in the lounge, glad to escape the hot sun for a while. Through the window I can see Freya talking to Judy. JP is still dealing with the barbeque, making me feel terribly guilty. Eventually Justin arrives with the ice-cold drinks. Taking the wet glass out of his hand I ask him to sit down with me. "I've applied for that job that you told me about," I inform him. "Let's hope you will get it," he replies, "Cheers!" "I haven't told Angie," I confess quickly. "Why not?" Justin wants to know. "She doesn't want to move. She doesn't want to go to Devon," I respond, emptying my glass of beer as if it is going out of fashion. Justin laughs. "It's no distance – you could almost commute and Devon is just like Cornwall. What's the difference? You'll have a better post, earn more money - what's the problem?" My face remains blank. "She wants to stay where her parents are, her friends are. Her argument is that at least she's got her family around when I am working long hours and going off to play golf at the weekends," I explain. I am about to mention the solicitor's letter I have received earlier when Angie marches up to us.

"I cannot believe you two are in here chatting and everyone else is outside wanting to see you. It's your party, Rob. I don't know what has got into you!" my wife tells us in no uncertain terms. Obediently we take our by now empty glasses and follow her into the back garden.

Angie has decided that it is time for cutting the cake so everyone is wishing me a happy birthday and I try – and fail – to blow the 40 candles out in one go. After that Justin and I persuade JP to join the football team. Jordan and Tom beg Judy to play because according to my son "Mum is useless at football". Justin's sexy girlfriend agrees immediately but I am a little concerned about her gorgeous dress and strappy sandals. Holding on to Melanie who is getting quite excited about the game Angie and Freya watch us play.

We are having fun but I can definitely feel dark clouds hanging over my marriage. Angie is still very angry with me and Jordan's comment about her non-existing football skills has not gone down well with her either. To the sheer delight of the boys Judy, now playing in bare feet, gets stuck in and scores several goals. JP, being the oldest, is our goalie but he soon throws the towel. "You youngsters are too good for me," he complains bitterly. Tom, in the opposing goal, shrugs his shoulders. He has defended Justin's hard shots heroically and is proud to be on the winning team. "OK, this is the end of the match," I announce quickly. "Time for a drink!"

Judy's feet are absolutely black and her hair is looking a little untidy but she smiles happily. She is cuddling into Justin and all I can think is: "You lucky thing!" I am convinced that the beer has gone to my head. Why am I feeling so envious? Dismissing my jealousy I load another by now rather black and slightly cold sausage onto my plate and start to eat.

Soon JP and Freya decide to call it a day and go home. Melanie is crying. She is getting tired and therefore increasingly irritable. "Can Tom stay for a sleep-over?" Jordan wants to know from his mother. "Ask Dad," Angie replies, not even looking at Judy or attempting to discuss it with her. "Yes, it's OK with me," I answer casually. I can see Justin smiling. Who wouldn't want Tom's Mum all to themselves for the night? "Thank you. We'll come and pick Tom up around lunch time tomorrow if that's OK," Judy says to me. The boys are thrilled. Laughing and jumping with joy they return to the garden while Judy is taking the car keys off Justin so that she can drive him home. "Thanks for the party, Rob. See you tomorrow," my best mate says before thanking Angie who is struggling to contain a violently fighting Melanie. Then Judy and Justin wave to Tom and leave our premises.

I am getting ready to give my wife a hand with our daughter but Angie just disappears upstairs without talking to me. Checking all around me like a thief I pull the envelope out of my jeans again and once more I read about my inheritance.

After a long struggle Angie has managed to put Melanie to sleep. She returns to the garden where the boys and I are tidying up. "I think you should ring Charles and apologise to him, Rob," she tells me, her face looking serious. "What for? It was about time that someone told him the truth. He drives us all mad with his permanent sales talk," I reply defiantly.

"Charles and Barbara are our friends. You can't treat them like this. I want you to apologise, even if you don't like it," Angie insists. Tom and Jordan look at each other, no doubt guessing that things are not great between Mum and Dad.

"Let's talk about it later," I suggest lamely. Realising that the boys are listening, Angie nods and turns away. "My Mum was always arguing with my Dad before he moved out," Tom tells us as we continue cleaning the barbeque. Jordan assesses the situation quietly for a while. "I don't want my Dad to move out though," he decides eventually. I try to ignore the boys' conversation but something inside me makes me cringe.

It is not until we go to bed that Angie and I find time to speak to each other in private. "I didn't think much of your behaviour today, Rob. It was really embarrassing," Angie starts. She is not touching me, keeping to her side of the bed deliberately. "I'm sorry," I respond, almost automatically. "I don't believe you are. You have refused to apologise to my friends, our friends. You wouldn't even do it to please me," Angie argues. It would be so easy to say "Fine, I'll do it tomorrow" but those words simply do not come over my lips. "I've been asked if everything is OK with us. People have obviously noticed the tension," Angie continues. "I'm sorry," I say again. I know it's not what Angie wants to hear right now but it just comes spontaneously. "We are not OK, are we? Ever since Melanie was born things haven't been right," Angie suddenly complains. My hand is reaching out for hers but she pulls it away. "I don't want to lose you, Rob but I've never been so unhappy in all my life," she explains, sounding terribly close to tears. "Perhaps we should make a new start…," I suggest foolishly. "A new start? Moving away – that's all you've ever wanted. Take me away from my family, the people who care about me and the children. A new start would mean changing schools for Jordan, now that he has settled in so well here. No, Rob, you know we mustn't do that. If we can't make our relationship work here we won't do it anywhere," Angie says sternly, still bravely fighting tears. I take a deep breath. "Tell me what it is that makes you so unhappy," I demand, once again daring to touch her. Angrily she pushes me away. "I don't know, can't put my finger on it. Sometimes it seems to me that we are just two people sharing this house. There is no love…," she tries to explain. Her words hurt. She is spelling out the truth.

"So what do you suggest we do to revive our love – and don't say have another baby because that is quite obviously not the answer," I retort uneasily. My wife's tears are in full flow now. "Nothing, Rob. There's nothing we can do. I still love you but if you don't love me back, what's the point?" she cries, withdrawing herself from my last attempt to have physical contact with her.

I have no answer to this. Deeply concerned about our future I roll over to my side and try to digest what I've just been told. Under no circumstances can I mention my application for the post in Devon or the letter advising me of my estranged aunt's death and my subsequent inheritance. I simply lie here, feeling numb until my mind takes me away into the world of forbidden thoughts. Suddenly I imagine Judy and Justin experiencing a night full of passion and pleasure. When was the last time we had anything like that? A very, very long time ago – I can't even remember when, if ever. My heart is beating like a drum. I decide to keep my secrets until I fall asleep.

In the morning, at the breakfast table, we are all smiling. The boys have had a good night and they are determined to drag us to the beach before lunch. "There's hardly enough time," Angie states, looking at her watch. "It's OK. I'll give Justin a ring and ask him and Judy to come a bit later," I suggest immediately. Angie leaves the table to get Melanie dressed and I make the call.

The weather is fantastic again. As I drive along with my wife sitting next to me and the three children in the back I think how lucky I am. I have a job that I love, a comfortable home, good friends and a great little family but then, seconds later, I feel that there is something missing. Concentrating on the traffic ahead of me I try to ignore the painful longing for adventure and excitement.

It is not often that I have a whole weekend off so I am really enjoying myself. Jordan, Tom and I are brave enough to take a dip in the North Cornish sea but the water is by far too cold for Angie and Melanie. Mother and daughter have set up camp at a safe spot on Bude's wide golden beach. From the distance it seems as if they are having fun but I have noticed that Angie has looked very sad and tense on the way here. Splashing about with the boys my mind wanders and I ask myself if I still love her or not. Instinctively my eyes follow her silhouette on the beach. She's in Bermuda shorts and a t-shirt whereas other women are wearing bikinis. "Dad, watch out," I hear Jordan's voice but it is too late. A large wave is crashing over my head. For seconds it buries me in a swirling mixture of sand and water, making me gasp for air as I resurface. "Are you OK?" Tom asks me kindly. "Yes, Tom, yes, absolutely fine," I reply untruthfully. I am reluctant to admit defeat but I've had enough. The tide has come in considerably and the wind has increased with it. Still trying to clear sand and salt out of my ears and hair I stagger back to the beach.

Angie is sitting on our big beach towel looking bored. I can tell that she is thinking about us. "You must be freezing," she states as I sit down next to her. Then she leans over to our bag to get another dry towel out for me. "Thanks," I say, wrapping myself up as fast as I can. Melanie has crawled off. She is exploring a neighbouring beach towel that has been spread out not far from us. I am not sure if the young couple lying on it find it quite as amusing as she does. Decisively I get up to bring my daughter back to our quarters. Angie's face appears strained. "We mustn't stay too long," she remarks, not looking at me as she speaks. I make no comment but I get dressed quickly as I am feeling chilly now. The boys are still in the water, totally oblivious to the cold. Pulling my polo shirt over my head I notice the young couple next to us kissing and cuddling. Angie is right, since we've had Melanie our sex life has gone downhill rapidly. "Two people sharing a house, a bed - but no love," were Angie's words last night. Bearing this in mind I move closer to my wife and put my arm around her. I can feel how tense she is but at least she is not pushing me away. Melanie has discovered the art of throwing hands full of sand around and she is laughing at her new skill. "I still love you," I whisper, hoping that my words will spark something off in her but Angie shakes her head. "I wish I could believe you, Rob," she says sadly. Very gently I kiss her hair. "Listen, if you are still sulking because of what I said to Charles yesterday I'll ring him up and apologise," I offer generously. Just as I've made my concession the boys return from the water. Both are shivering, covered in goose pimples from head to toe. "When you are dressed we'll have a jog along the beach to warm up," I suggest smiling. "No such thing," Angie contradicts. "We'll have to go home. Judy and Justin will be waiting," she insists.

Less than half an hour later we are back in the car. The boys are lively but Angie's mood has not changed. She is unusually quiet on the journey home. Melanie has fallen asleep, giving us a break from her baby chatter. As we arrive we find Justin's car parked outside our house, however my best mate is not around. "He's been called into work," Judy explains. Tom is pleased to see his mother, storming into her arms. "Oh dear, you are cold as ice," she remarks, rubbing his slim arms. I ask her in for a drink. "No, thank you, Rob. I'd like to get going as soon as possible. I've promised to pick Justin up on the way back," she declines. Then she thanks Angie and Jordan. Within minutes she has left.

I feel obliged to ring Charles now. Being used to difficult customers certainly helps with handling this awkward situation. As Barbara answers the phone I immediately make my apologies to her and it seems that she is prepared to forgive me but Charles simply refuses to speak to me. My call causes quite a row between the two of them. I have to listen to the domestic crises at the other end of the phone line and smile to myself. "Don't worry," I tell Barbara eventually. "Just tell him that I am truly sorry for what I've said and that I'll ask him around for a couple of beers soon," I offer graciously. Heaving a sigh of relief I finally return to Angie who is preparing food in the kitchen. "All done," I report proudly. "Thank you," replies my wife rather formally but she is not smiling. Melanie has woken up and demands my attention.

As the evening approaches I am seriously considering talking to Angie about my job application and the inheritance but she decides to go and see her parents. She leaves me in charge of getting our children to bed. I really enjoy being a father but at this moment in time I am not so sure about my role as a husband.

Pouring myself a beer I sit up waiting for Angie to return, still wondering if I can a) bring myself to tell her about my plans for the future and b) persuade her to make love to me tonight. Forgetting the time I am almost asleep on the sofa when Angie comes back. She is surprised to see me sitting downstairs. "I didn't expect you to be still up," she says. "It's late and I thought you'd gone to bed," she adds. Rubbing my eyes I am wondering if she has talked to her parents about her recent unhappiness. She is certainly looking pale, just tired perhaps. "Come here and sit down with me for a bit," I invite her. "Don't you know what the time is, Rob? You've got to be at work at eight," she remarks, not taking the seat I offer her. "There is something I'd like to discuss with you," I tell her then. Her sad face is looking concerned now. I can feel that I can write off any intimacy with her once I've let the cat out of the bag. At least she is sitting down, well away from me though. Taking a very deep breath I say: "I have applied for a job in Plymouth." Her head bowed Angie replies: "I had a strange feeling that you were harbouring something inside. Why didn't you tell me before?" "Who knows if I'll get it anyway and it's just across the border, no big deal," I answer feebly. "It's a big deal for me, Rob. You are starting to do things behind my back. I would hate to join the sad statistics of failed marriages but we are heading that way," she says. "Even if I am being offered the job I don't have to take it – and we don't have to move. It's in Derriford, just a few miles down the road," I explain bravely. For the first time in ages my wife looks at me properly, her eyes meeting mine. There is an uncomfortable pause before she says: "I know you've wanted to move on for some time now but even if it is just across the border it will mean that you will be away from home even more. Have you ever considered that I might like to go back to work as well?" "Once Melanie is old enough for play school I can see no reason why you shouldn't," I reply but I have to admit that I have not taken Angie's career into account.

Without any further discussion she gets up and walks away, leaving me feel like a fool. The fact that I have not talked to her before completing my application has upset her by far more than the fact that I may take up a post in Devon. Although I realise that I have deeply disappointed her I resolve not to tell her about my inheritance until I've been to see the cottage for myself.

Needless to say there was no chance of a physical reunion last night but this morning I am feeling quite excited about going to work. I have got the solicitor's letter in my briefcase and I can't wait to get in touch with the firm. My colleague Jackie is busy with customers for most of the morning, so I have plenty of time for private phone calls.

I still can't believe that my aunt has left the cottage to me. She was my Dad's only sister, quite a bit older and very eccentric. Dad and Delia fell out when I was about fifteen. All I know is that she married a rich mining specialist and moved to Australia. As far as I am aware she never had any children and my parents had just me. It never occurred to me that she could own a property in Cornwall. My Dad who died three years ago never had a decent word to say about his sister. I don't think that she even knew that he has passed away. My mother certainly never mentioned informing her of Dad's death. Well, I didn't know of her death either – until now.

During the morning I eventually get hold of the gentleman who is dealing with my aunt's affairs. He seems pleased that I am at least considering accepting Delia's bequest. "We understand that the house is currently being let through a local agent. I'll get in touch with them and ask them to contact you. Once we have received all your identification papers we can make arrangements for you to see the property," the friendly legal executive offers. He urges me to send the necessary documents to his office in London as soon as possible and I advise him to address any future correspondence to my attention at the car dealership where I work rather than home.

The next few days and nights I can do nothing but sit back and wait – wait to hear about my job application, wait for Angie to show me some affection, wait for further details from the solicitors. Still, my little secret provides me with some kind of excitement.

It's late on a Friday afternoon when I eventually receive a phone call from the letting agent in Newquay. "I've spoken to the tenants who are in your property at present. They are happy for you to come and have a look at it any time you like," the agent tells me. I have to think about that. First of all I need Jackie to be around that day so that I can take time off from work and then I need to make up some excuse why I have to go away for the day. Telling the agent that I am going to ring him back I buy myself a little time to get matters sorted. Jackie is prepared to let me have a day off on Wednesday so I go for that date.

When I get home that evening Angie hands me a letter from the Mercedes dealership in Devon. I have been invited to attend an interview on Thursday afternoon which amazingly fits in fine with my plans. "Well done, good luck," Angie says as she serves our dinner but I sense that she is not really happy for me. "I am afraid I won't be around much on Wednesday either," I inform her. "I've got to attend a meeting in Newquay. Hopefully it won't last too long though. If it's OK with you I may pop in to see Justin on the way back," I add quickly. "You do what you like, Rob. I have decided to move into Melanie's room for a while. We can't go on pretending that we are a happy couple," she says plainly. Suddenly I've lost my appetite. With my fork aimlessly circling around the plate in front of me I realise that Angie is taking the first step towards a separation. "Have you told Jordan?" I ask. "Yes, in fact he helped me put the guest bed up when he came home from school. I've told him it's because of Melanie. He knows that she wakes up in the middle of the night sometimes and I told him that it is easier for me to see to her," Angie explains. I nod uneasily.

Interestingly enough I sleep really well the first night on my own in our bedroom. I would have put money on it that I would be missing my wife next to me but I do not. On Saturday morning I go to work feeling quite relaxed but deep inside I am a worried man. The prospect of a separation does not suit me at all. I am determined to get things back on track before it is too late. Just before leaving work that afternoon I ring Justin. He works at his parents' prestigious Jaguar dealership near Bodmin. Debating whether to tell him where I am planning to go on Wednesday or not I nervously step from one foot to the other. Eventually I ask him: "Are you going to be around on Wednesday afternoon? I've got a meeting in Newquay. Perhaps I could come and see you for a few minutes on the way home." Then I tell him about the interview on Thursday. Needless to say he is pleased for me, genuinely, I mean. He agrees to meet me at his office just after 5pm, and I have to say I am looking forward to it.

Angie and I are getting on fairly well over the weekend so the children don't realise what is going on. I have not managed to persuade Angie to return to the marital bed though. She insists that we need a bit of distance from each other but am not convinced that she is entirely satisfied with the current situation. At times I am hopeful that we will soon be back to normal. Personally, I think I am working very hard on making our marriage work again.

Luckily Angie has not asked what meeting I am going to on Wednesday. She just accepts that it is part of my job. Once I am in the car on the way to the famous tourist resort I feel incredibly excited. My cottage is located in a small seaside village just outside of Newquay by the name of Crantock. I don't think that I've ever been there before but it sounds very quaint. Unfortunately, the weather is terrible. It has not stopped raining since I've left home. My appointment with the letting agent is at 11am. He has told me exactly how to get to my cottage and I have no difficulties finding it. In this weather the village doesn't look quite as pretty as in the pictures that I have seen on the internet but still, it is well away from the busy holiday resort of Newquay but close enough for properties to offer great letting potential.

I am a little early so I park my car by the road side and wait for the agent to arrive. The cottage is right in the middle of the village. From the outside it seems quite small and in urgent need of updating. There is a tiny garden in the front which certainly requires attention. Despite the heavy rain I eventually get out of the car to have a good look around. Curiously I inspect the windows, the paint work, the walls and the gutters. "Hi, you must be Mr Cunningham," a friendly voice suddenly says behind me. Instantly I turn around. "Yes, and you are?" I say to the figure under the most enormous black rain jacket. "I'm Beth, Beth Henderson, nice to meet you," the wet lips under the coat tell me. "Alan will be here in a minute. Please, do come in,"

Beth invites me. She is searching in her oversized coat for the keys. Then she lets me enter my property. My first impression is that it is damp and the floor boards are creaking horribly. Beth takes her large coat off. She smiles at me and I have to admit that I like the look of her. "Please do come through," she says, her fingers combing through her short brown hair. She's wearing tight jeans and a polo shirt. I follow her to the lounge. "I am sorry that it is so untidy," she apologises. We have to step over maps, books and loose sheets of paper. "The reason for this mess is that I am writing a book and I like to spread myself out, as you can see," she explains. Apart from an old sofa, two armchairs that have seen better days, a terribly scratched coffee table and a poor-quality wooden cupboard there is no furniture in the room. To be honest I find the place a bit depressing. "Right, I'll show you the kitchen now. I've got to put my shopping away," Beth says. She is not very tall but she's well built, in fact she looks extremely fit. I follow her, not saying anything.

The kitchen is absolutely miniscule. A cooker, one cupboard, a tiny fridge and a couple of wonky chairs fill the room up completely. "I think it would be possible to create a decent kitchen if one spent a bit of money and knocked the wall down," Beth comments, her strong small fingers touching the grimy wall in front of her. I have not said a word but she must be able to read my mind. "OK, that's all down here. I'll show you upstairs…," she starts but at that moment we hear a voice at the door. It is Alan from the letting agency. "I'm about to show Mr Cunningham around upstairs," Beth tells the ginger-haired man with thickly-framed glasses. "Fine, carry on," Alan agrees. We climb up the narrow stairs to the first floor. "Bedroom 1 – the master bedroom," Beth explains, opening the door to a surprisingly large room. In it is a modern double bed, a wide wardrobe and a desk complete with sophisticated computer equipment. "I spend most of my time up here writing. The light is good and I like this room the best," she tells me and Alan who is following on. Then we enter bedroom 2, a much smaller but also quite pleasant room. There is a simple single bed with bedside cabinet, an old wardrobe, a dressing table and a small portable TV. Next to the single room there is a fairly well equipped bathroom. "Right, that's it really. The cottage has a loft space but I've never been up there," Beth says, looking at Alan. I am still standing in bedroom 2, watching huge rain drops banging onto the old windows. My mind is wandering. "As you can see, the whole house needs updating but it has a lot of potential," Alan disturbs my day-dreams. Beth has already noticed that I am not impressed. "We love it here. The beach is wonderful, people are friendly and the village is so quiet," she says, again smiling at me.

I am trying hard to come back to reality. "So how long have you rented the cottage for?" I ask her. "Unfortunately, we've got to go back on 31st August," Beth replies. "I've had some enquiries for the first week in September already though," Alan pops up proudly. "Last year I was able to let it all through the winter as well," he adds quickly. I nod, not sure what to say. "Let's go downstairs and I'll show you some figures," Alan offers. Beth is making us a cup of tea while Alan and I discuss the income and expenditure for my cottage. It's all a little bit beyond me but I listen and learn as I go along. "If you would like to sell it my husband will put an offer in, I am quite sure," Beth suddenly says. Alan smiles. "Yes, Mr Henderson has spoken to me about it before he left for Canada," he confirms eagerly. I am in a win-win situation here but I am not prepared to make a decision yet.

"Well, I've got to go to another appointment now. You know where we are, Mr Cunningham. Very nice to have met you and no doubt you will let me know soon what you are planning to do with the property," Alan says and shakes my hand. "Feel free to have another good look around. It's too wet to go to the garden at the moment but it's great out there in fine weather," Beth tells me. We say good-bye to Alan but I stay on. "While you are looking around I'll make a couple of sandwiches. It's way past my lunch time," Beth says. She seems a lovely woman. That Mr Henderson, whoever he might be, is a lucky man, I think as I wander through the cottage. Minutes later I find myself sitting on the ancient sofa, Beth Henderson next to me in the worn-out armchair and we are having lunch. She asks me about my aunt, my background and my family. We talk freely as if we'd known each other for a long time. The way she looks at me makes me wonder if she likes me, too. She tells me about her book, her husband and her two sons who are spending the summer holidays in America with friends. "Brian and I have the same problem as you – this place is by far too small for four people but…," and with that she gets up and walks over to the window. "Brian has made enquiries. There is a chance that the cottage can be extended, shame to lose the garden though." Taking my sandwich with me I follow her. Through the wet glass we can see the long piece of land behind my property. "I've no intention of living here," I suddenly say. Beth smiles sweetly. "Well, just a thought," she comments apologetically.

It has stopped raining so she leads me outside. I am surprised how large the back garden really is. "It's a valuable property, I think. Brian and I have looked at a couple of other houses around here. They are very expensive for what they are but then, Crantock is just magic," Beth says. Looking at my watch I decide that it is time for me to leave. I have no reason to stop her from doing her work any longer. "Good luck with your book. I will be in touch with Alan when I've had time to consider all the facts and figures," I say to her. "Nice to have met you, Mr Cunningham. Why don't you bring your family down to see the cottage? You don't need to ask Alan. Here's my number. Just ring me or send me a text if you want to come to view the cottage again. Brian is away until the end of August and I am here most of the time," Beth offers. "Thanks – also for the lunch – and please call me Rob," I reply. Waving her good-bye I jump in my car and drive off.

Once I have reached the main road my head starts spinning. I will have to talk to Justin about my inheritance. If I want to continue keeping the cottage a secret I will need his help. Feeling a little dizzy I stop in a lay-by to sit back and gather my thoughts. The cottage would be an ideal hide-away, a place where I can be on my own if things are getting tough. Yet again checking the time I pull my papers for tomorrow's interview out of my briefcase in readiness for some mental preparation. As hard as I try I find it difficult to concentrate. Eventually it is time to move on and I drive, admittedly a little too fast, towards the elegant showroom where Justin works.

As I enter the large hall where the highly polished luxury cars are parked up under bright spotlights I have second thoughts about sharing my secret with him. "What meeting have you been to, Rob? You look totally washed out," my friend remarks. He has left his super-clean office to greet me. "I'll tell you all about it in the pub," I reply. Helping him lock up I can feel my heartbeat picking up pace. We walk over to the King's Arms where Justin orders the drinks. I drop into one of the heavy leather chairs, out of ear shot of the bar maid. When Justin returns with two pints of lager I put the creased-up solicitor's letter on the table for him to read. "Wow, congratulations! Cheers!" he says happily once he has studied the contents. My facial expression remains strained. Looking around carefully as if to avoid being heard by others I say: "I don't want Angie to know." "Have you been to see it yet?" Justin asks and he sounds excited. "That's where I've been today," I admit lamely. All of a sudden the well-tanned Justin stops smiling. "Hang on – you haven't told Angie about the job in Devon and you don't want her to know about this. What's going on, Rob? Doesn't sound good to me," he says. "I have told Angie about my application now and that I've been invited for an interview," I start but then I pause. Justin takes a sip of lager waiting for me to explain myself. "Well, I don't want her to know about the cottage just yet. Frankly, I am not quite sure what to do with it," I say slowly. "So what is it like?" Justin wants to know. "Old, small, in need of work but as I understand it the place is a pretty good source of income," I reply nervously. "OK, so why don't you want to show it to Angie?" Justin asks. Nervously I begin to play with my pint glass. "Angie and I – we are going through a bit of a rough patch at the moment," I finally confess. "Sorry to hear that," Justin comments but he does not say anything else. "I'd like to keep the cottage a secret – at least until I've decided what to do," I tell him. "There are tenants in it until 31st August but after that date I could use it...," I add. "But even if you get the job in Devon, isn't it too far away for you to live there?" Justin asks. "Yes, it is too far for work I suppose but it would be great for weekends, as a project for me. I fancy doing it up, bit by bit," I explain, getting a little carried away. Justin shakes his head. "You sound as if you are divorced already," he remarks bluntly.

This is the first time the horrible d-word has been mentioned and it hurts immensely. I don't want to get divorced. How dare Justin think our relationship has come to an end this quickly? "Please, Justin. Will you help me keep my inheritance a secret for a while?" I ask him straight out. My friend shrugs his broad shoulders. "Yes, sure," he replies casually. "Thanks, that's great. I may have to tell Angie that I am with you from time to time when I want to see the cottage. Is that OK?" I enquire carefully. "You are playing a dangerous game, Rob. I'm not sure if I like it," Justin says now. "Please, Justin, just for a few weeks until I know what's happening," I plead with him. "OK," he finally submits. We finish our pints. Soon it is time for me to make my way home. Justin sees me off, wishing me luck for the interview tomorrow and then I return home to Launceston.

"You look as if you've had a tough day," Angie tells me over dinner that evening. The children are in bed and I really appreciate that she has waited for me with some food. "You can imagine what it was like – all that talk and then nothing but listen, listen, listen at these meetings," I lie easily. Angie smiles. She is trying to be understanding. "Have you decided if you will accept the job tomorrow if they offer it to you?" she asks then. "If they want me I shall go for it," I answer, sounding very determined. Angie is not happy and I know it. Admittedly, the thought of getting up even earlier every morning and returning home later, particularly in the summer, is not an appealing thought but it is a small price to pay for a better post and higher remuneration.

I offer to help Angie with the dishes but she sends me off to bed. "You will want to be at your best tomorrow. I've rarely seen you look so tired when you've been away," she says. Obediently I get ready, wondering what would happen if I invited Angie to join me in our bed but then I decide that maybe it is not the right night to try it.

Having to be at work the next morning before attending an interview in the afternoon is not a good idea. I feel strangely nervous, not myself at all. After lunch I go home to get changed. Once I am dressed Angie inspects me critically from head to toe. She says I look very presentable. She even stops me from handling Melanie, just in case she accidentally makes my suit dirty. "Good luck," my wife says as I am leaving the house but she fails to kiss me like she used to before I went off anywhere.

Driving along towards Plymouth I have doubts over my preparation for the interview. I am generally a confident person, comfortable with giving presentations, answering questions and I dare say I have been in the job long enough to know what to expect but today I feel unsure about absolutely everything.

As I arrive in the car park of the brand-new Mercedes dealership, just outside of Plymouth, my mind is again wandering. Rather than thinking about the task ahead I consider my options for the cottage. Very slowly, by my standards, I leave my car and walk over to the vast steel and glass construction which houses the state-of-the-art showroom. It does not look as if there are any other applicants around but I can't be sure. I get little chance to take a good look at the stunning new cars as the Managing Director, a tall man in his late fifties, catches up with me. He sounds as if he's known me for many years. "Rob, great to see you. Please, do come in," he invites me.

In the sterile-looking conference room I am being introduced to several members of staff. Some of them are smiling, others not. Everyone is pretending to be friendly though, making me feel reasonably comfortable. I try my best to impress them and answer all their questions. Time is flying until all of a sudden it's over. The Managing Director invites me for a coffee afterwards. "We will have a discussion about your appointment later this evening. Then we will give you a call tomorrow," he tells me. It appears that they are not going to see many, if any, other candidates. This surprises me. "Thank you, that's fine with me," I reply politely. We are having a good chat about the latest models of Mercedes before I decide that I must return home.

I have visited Plymouth quite a few times so the surroundings are familiar to me but the thought of working here in the near future still feels odd. Anyway, I drive back to Launceston only to find a note from Angie that she and the children have gone to visit her parents this evening. So I am home alone, thinking about when I can escape to the cottage again. I put my laptop on when suddenly I have an idea. Didn't Justin say he was going to have an Open Day at his dealership on Sunday? My diary tells me that Sunday will be my day off this week. How about telling Angie that Justin has asked me to come along? She wouldn't think that there is anything strange about that. I could leave really early, drive straight to the cottage, spend most of the day exploring the area, measuring up, looking around. It would give me a welcome break from family life and work. I like the idea a lot so I quickly send an e-mail to Justin.

Luckily he responds almost instantly. He says that he would prefer it if I really did come to see him at the Open Day but fortunately he is prepared to cover up for me which is kind of him. To be on the safe side I delete our correspondence immediately. Then I pick up my mobile and ring Beth Henderson. She sounds very pleased to hear from me. "Sunday? Yes, perfect. Will you bring your family? The weather forecast is good for Sunday," she tells me excitedly. "It'll only be me again. I am just popping in to take some measurements if that's OK," I reply. "Great. What time will you be arriving?" Beth wants to know. "Early, say nine or 9.30am?" I suggest. "Fantastic. I'll be here," Beth says. As I have used my mobile she will now have my number which I have not given her before. So if there should be any problems she can get in touch with me. Once again I get rid of any evidence of the phone call. Then I begin to relax.

Angie, Jordan and Melanie return at 8pm. They have had a meal with my parents-in-law but Angie says she's going to make me something to eat now and she also enquires how I got on at the interview. I volunteer to see to the children. As I am changing Melanie's nappy Jordan joins me in her room. "Dad, Mummy has been talking to Gran. She said something about not wanting to be with you anymore," he tells me. I almost drop Melanie who is wriggling like a worm on the changing mat. At this minute I don't know what to say to that. Poor Jordan demands an answer but I have none. I find this situation an awful lot more difficult than being grilled by an interview panel. Sighing I say: "Look, Jordan. Mum and I have had an argument. These things happen. You fall out with your friends from time to time, don't you? We will make up soon, I am sure." I can tell from looking at his face that Jordan is not convinced. All I can think of is very quickly changing the subject, so for something to say I describe to my son all the new Mercedes cars I have seen today.

Melanie is teething. She is really troublesome tonight. Both Angie and I are trying to settle her down but she wakes up every half hour, crying. At least Jordan has gone to bed without any further questions. "I am going to see Justin at his Open Day on Sunday. It will be good to learn how Jaguar organise these events," I inform my wife. She nods sadly. "We are seeing less and less of you these days. Please don't dcny it, Rob. You are looking for excuses to be away from me, away from us, your family. Tell me the truth. Do you want us to formally separate?" she asks. "No, definitely not.

I want us to be together again. This is crazy. I want you to move back into our bed. I want us to be a normal married couple again," I protest strongly. "Sleeping together is not going to solve any problems," Angie states sternly. I don't agree. "It's a start…," I say. My wife shakes her head. "You men always think sex is everything," she remarks indignantly. "I meant what I told you on the beach. I love you and I want to share my life and my bed with you," I tell her, reaching out for her hand. I am making a huge effort here. Will I get a reward?

Melanie is stirring again, whimpering in her cot. Angie gets up and goes upstairs to check up on her. I am left sitting on the sofa, my hands covering my face, realising that we may well have reached the end of the road. Not wanting to give up without a fight I follow Angie. I am expecting to find her in Melanie's room but instead she's in the bathroom crying. She's locked herself in. All I can do is plead with her to come out and talk to me. I am so ready to comfort her but I feel like a silly schoolboy, knocking on the bathroom door. Angie is no longer the only one who is not happy. I am more than unhappy with the current state of affairs, too.

Once I've coaxed my wife out of the bathroom she decides that she doesn't want to be comforted by me. She spends the night in Melanie's room as usual. I feel quite hurt about that so when I go to work the next morning I am not in the best frame of mind.

I receive the call at around 10am. The job in Plymouth is mine if I want it. Naturally, I am delighted and accept. Having confided in Jackie before, I make her the first person to know about my success. My dear colleague cannot even bring herself to smile. "I will miss you, Rob, just can't imagine working here without you," she says, sounding upset. "I will miss you too," I respond immediately and that is the truth. Jackie and I have always got on well but when the time comes to move on I must take my chances, I decide. There is now an awful lot of paperwork to do – handing in my notice, writing a formal letter of acceptance, conveying the news to customers and my colleagues in the workshop and so on. Jackie insists that I must have a farewell party. She is already making plans and scribbling things down on a note pad. With my private life in tatters I can't properly enjoy this feeling of pride, of having achieved something.

Only a couple of days have passed but rumours about the reasons for my departure are spreading like wildfire. I am on the phone all morning and every single customer expresses their sadness that I am leaving but most of them are wishing me well in my new job, too. In the afternoon the workshop manager arrives at my office to see me. He has only just been told that I won't be here anymore after 1st September.

A little later than usual I eventually arrive at home, full of mixed emotions.

"I've got the job," I announce to Angie, hoping that she will be pleased for me but she simply nods. "Congratulations," she says rather formally. I feel like cracking open a bottle of champagne so I offer to go out to buy one. "Don't bother, Rob. I am not going to celebrate with you. I've been to see a solicitor today," she tells me. It's a shock, a real, terrible shock to hear that. Totally devastated I drop down into the sofa. I haven't even noticed that the children are not around. "It's better this way. We must both start a new life," Angie explains. In my head everything is going haywire. I feel like ringing Plymouth to turn the job down. I want to take Angie into my arms and shake her, ask her to wake up and come to her senses. I want to run away, go for a drive, get drunk. I don't know what I want but in reality I just sit here, feeling sorry for myself. Then it dawns on me. "Where are the kids?" I ask. "Next door, with Freya," Angie replies. "I did not want Jordan to hear our conversation about the separation," she adds. This has got to be the worst day of my life.

The next couple of hours pass very clinically. Angie agrees that we will continue living under one roof while I am working out my notice but after that she wants me to find myself some accommodation in Plymouth and move out. We are talking about splitting up our possessions, arrangements for seeing the children, financial matters. The pain inside of me is getting unbearable. I don't want this, none of it. All I want to do is cry. The whole affair is so depressing. "Please, Angie, stop. Do we really have to do this?" I finally shout. My wife nods. "Yes, I think so," she whispers.

33

Eventually Angie goes next door to fetch the children. We have agreed not to tell Jordan until tomorrow night but the way he looks at me at dinner time tells me that he is guessing something is up. I am now seriously considering cancelling my plans to visit the cottage and spend Sunday with the kids. It is hard to describe how much I am hurting, to think that all this may soon be over. According to Angie I will only see my children every two weeks or so.

Once Melanie and Jordan are in bed Angie offers to open a bottle of wine. "We can both do with a drop," she suggests and she is right. She gets the glasses and I open the bottle. "They were a wedding gift," I comment as I am passing her a glass. "You can have them if you like," Angie says. Her words make me swear. I tell her in no uncertain terms that I don't want the glasses but that I want her. Something in my head is exploding and I start losing it completely. I am beside myself with anger. Angie tells me to stop. She does not want me to wake the children up but I just rant on until she takes her glass and leaves the lounge to go upstairs. Her action makes me come to my senses. I sit down, all by myself now, and drink the rest of the bottle. By midnight my macho-man mask falls and I cry.

Angie has been crying too. She tells me so when she wakes me up on the sofa the next morning. I am feeling most embarrassed as Jordan comes down the stairs to find me fully dressed in yesterday's clothes in the lounge. "Dad fell asleep on the sofa last night," Angie explains. I can detect a hint of a smile on her face. Jordan shrugs his shoulders and sits down at the breakfast table while I make my apologies and go upstairs to take a shower.

Honestly, I can't remember ever being late for work but I am this morning. "Well, well, standards are slipping now that you are going to leave us," Jackie says jokingly as I walk in, full of excuses. I hate being late. On top of that I am hung over which is not a good feeling either. In today's post I receive a great number of good-luck and farewell cards. There is no end to the messages and wishes from all kinds of people I have worked with for the last few years. It is all quite moving but also extremely painful.

In my lunch break I finally manage to ring Justin. He is thrilled that I got the job and obviously sorry to hear about my domestic problems. "I'm not sure if I want to go ahead with Sunday," I tell him. "If not, I'll let you know. I am so confused, it's unreal," I admit. Justin has experience with splitting up, although, of course, he's never been married – must be much easier, I think. We have a short conversation about golf and that's it. Still, I am grateful that he listens and wants to remain friends with me. He is just about the only person I can trust at the moment.

When I get home from work both my mother and my parents-in-law are sitting in the lounge waiting for me. Angie's parents are offering to take Jordan away with them for the weekend and my Mum says that she's happy to have Melanie all day tomorrow or Sunday. Surprisingly Jordan is dead keen on visiting Lundy Island with his grandparents but Angie insists that she would prefer to keep Melanie for the weekend. "She's teething, it's not a good time," she explains to my mother. My Mum has not been in the best of health lately so I agree that it would be sensible not to leave Melanie with her. The older generation finds it hard to accept that we are separating. I've told my Mum that I don't want to divorce Angie but I know that my wife's parents are backing her up all the way.

Jordan has gone upstairs to pack his bags while I am in the kitchen helping Angie to prepare some food for the crowd in the living room. We don't normally cater for so many people. Soon Angie sends me out to the nearest supermarket to buy in more supplies. Quite unintentionally we end up having a bit of a party at home that night. I am ashamed to confess that I've been drinking heavily all evening. Luckily the older folk, plus young Jordan, make a move before it becomes too obvious that I am drunk. "Well, that went off OK," Angie remarks as we are clearing up. She has had one or two glasses of wine too. Melanie is in bed and we are doing the dishes. In my state of trance I don't realise that Angie is nervous. She is avoiding me but, of course, I don't notice it. As she is putting the plates away I put my arms around her, trying to kiss her. I don't think she has ever been afraid of me but she is now. Furiously she fights me off, telling me to leave her alone. We are starting to fight – and that's all I remember.

Early on Saturday morning I wake up to an empty house. Both Angie and Melanie have gone. Yet again I find myself fully dressed but I am in our bed in the bedroom. Don't ask me how I got there. I have to get a move on to get to work on time, and again I have a self-inflicted headache. Angie rings at around 11am. She informs me that she and Melanie will be staying with Barbara and Charles for the weekend. In a way that suits me fine. I ring Justin to confirm that I'll be making the trip to Crantock tomorrow after all and I have to force myself not to start drinking once I've left work.

After a lonely night I set off towards Crantock the next morning. I feel fine and even better when I realise that Beth's weather forecast is correct. It is a most beautiful Sunday. At this time of day the roads are still clear. I make incredibly good time. It's just after 9am when I arrive at my cottage. In the sunshine both the village and my property look so much nicer. Excitedly I ring the doorbell. It does not seem to be working so I knock. Beth rushes to let me in. She is looking absolutely stunning today. I am secretly wondering if she has deliberately dressed up for me. Her warm smile greets me before she begins to speak:"Hi, come in." The house is looking much tidier too, quite different from the last time.

"Have you had breakfast yet?" Beth asks me. "Just a bowl of cereal," I reply truthfully. "I am about to have mine. You can join me if you like," she says, leading me out onto the small patio at the back of the cottage. A small cast iron table is laid up ever so nicely. Apart from the old-fashioned but somehow charming crockery I spot a vase full of wild flowers in the middle. I feel quite sure that she has not laid this table for herself. "Please, take a seat. Tea or coffee?" she asks me. It is pleasantly warm in this sheltered area of the garden. Birds are singing in the neighbouring trees and I am instantly captured by the sweet potent fragrance of the roses in the surrounding flower beds. What a romantic place this is! I am opting for tea and that is what Beth is having as well. Minutes later we are starting a lively conversation. Beth does not stop smiling at me as she talks. She most definitely likes me. I can't explain it but I am feeling totally relaxed in her company. In her sophisticated summer dress she looks very sexy too. I am beginning to get a bit carried away here. "I can't understand why you haven't brought your family along today, Rob," I suddenly hear her say. My head bowed I decide that she is by far too gorgeous to be told lies so I answer: "My wife and I…," but then I can't continue. I can't bring myself to say it. "Oh, dear. I'm sorry," Beth says helplessly. While she seems to have read my thoughts immediately I am struggling to get back on track. "It's a tough time," I stutter. "Yes, of course. Let's change the subject. Tell me, what are your plans for the cottage?" she cleverly rectifies the awkwardness of the situation. I am unbelievably grateful for that. We get up and I show her what I am thinking of updating inside. Soon we are on our hands and knees measuring up. Beth is full of brilliant ideas – and best of all we are having such a laugh. Time flies like never before. "I'd like to invite you for lunch," I suddenly say, out of the blue. "Thank you. That's kind of you but first of all I must show you the beach. Did you say you've never seen it? Have you brought your swimming trunks?" she asks. I shake my head. "No problem. I expect I'll find one of Brian's here somewhere. You'll easily fit into them," Beth offers. Alarm bells are finally starting to ring. This is going a little too far for my liking. I am not prepared to wear another man's swimming trunks and go to the beach with his attractive wife. What next! I am a married man and she's a married woman – no way.

I am like glued to the spot but she runs swiftly up the stairs. Seconds later she returns with a couple of beach towels and a pair of super-funky boardies. "Brian doesn't like them. He's never worn them, I don't think," Beth tells me, holding the expensive-looking board shorts up in front of me. I can sense what she is thinking right now. Her eyes have already undressed me, even before she got the trunks down. She can see that I am most reluctant. "Hey, what's wrong? I bet they'll look great on you!" Well, there we are. That's what I mean. I knew it but I am surprised she is admitting it so openly. I cannot explain why but my hands reach out for the multi-coloured boardies. This makes Beth visibly happy. In the late morning heat we soon walk down the road towards the sea. Both large car parks near the popular beach are already packed. We walk uphill, through the hot and deep sand of a steep dune, until we can see the turquoise water in front of us. It is the most wonderful place. Alongside the vast golden beach a wide but perfectly calm river is inviting children to play on its banks. For a moment we watch them digging up the fine sand. The main beach is very busy already but there is plenty of space for everyone. We have taken our sandals off, marching through the heavy but beautifully soft sand. On our left we are passing the surf school with its colourful array of boards and wonky-looking clothes rail full of wetsuits, to the right there is an ice-cream kiosk. It's like being on holiday. Beth walks fast. She doesn't only look fit, she is fit. "Sorry, I haven't asked you if you can swim but considering that you were once a professional sportsman I have little doubt about it," Beth says. I had told her over breakfast that I started adult life on the national golf circuit but never earned enough prize money to make a living from it. Her words make me smile. "Yes, I can swim," I confirm, laughing. "And you look to me as if you are up for a challenge, right? Some people find the water cold but I absolutely love it," Beth tells me. She puts our towels down and starts undressing. I can't help watching her. She has a beautiful body. I feel immensely privileged to be on the beach with her.

Currently the tide is pretty far out. We have to walk a long way across a wide area of firm damp sand until we reach the water's edge. I am feeling very uncomfortable and a little self-conscious in Beth's husband's surfer shorts but the way she eyes me up from top to bottom she must think that I look acceptable. Her pace gathering speed she is waving to the lifeguards who seem to know her. Within seconds she is in the water, encouraging me to follow. It certainly is cold but I dare not make a fuss. *Straight in, Rob*, I tell myself and that's what I do. Seriously, the water is fantastic – so clear, so refreshing. I love it too. Beth is swimming along happily, keeping a watchful eye on me. "It's great, isn't it?" she enquires carefully. I have to agree. It really is out of this world. What I am feeling at this very moment is impossible to describe. I've lost all sense of reality - it's like in a dream. Beth is flirting with me and I like it.

We stay in the sea by far too long. Once we leave the water Beth makes me run back to our towels. "Just to warm you up," she assures me but I expect she is secretly testing my fitness. Despite the hot sunshine we have to put all our clothes back on to avoid shivering. Beth has stretched herself out on her beach towel. "So what exactly is your husband doing in Canada?" I want to know, sitting down next to her. "Working, of course. He's a businessman. He's always travelling. I was well aware of the fact that he would hardly ever be home when we got married. It suits me fine. Writing is a lonely job. I need peace and quiet. It's fine, honestly," she says, soaking up the warm sunshine. I am still sitting upright, staring at the vast ocean in the distance. "Lie down, relax a bit before we go out for lunch," Beth encourages me. I am not sure that I want to but I obey. "And what was it like being a golf pro? Brian is a member of a very exclusive club in London but he doesn't practice enough to be any good. He occasionally pays for lessons and afterwards all I hear is how amazing his teacher was!" Beth says. She has covered her face with her sun hat. Feeling strangely free I tell her about my struggles with professional golf, how much I prefer selling cars and earning a steady income and that I've just accepted a new job in Devon. It doesn't take long until I mention Angie and my children. Slowly Beth is rising from the towel. She is smiling, and I am finding it hard to keep my eyes off her. The last thing I want is her noticing how much she excites me. "Let's go and have a bite to eat," I suggest, not wanting to go into any further detail about my marriage either.

Chatting away we walk back into the village. I am beginning to understand why Beth likes it here so much. We end up sitting in the sunny beer garden of the local pub, talking like old friends. The more I look at Beth the more I like her. It scares me to think that I am starting to fancy her. "Before we go back to the cottage I'd like to show you the church. I am not a great believer but I love looking at old churches – and St Carantoc is well worth a visit," she says. So in the early afternoon we walk through the cemetery to the ancient Cornish church. Beth is right. It is a beautiful building, full of history. As we enter I am immediately fascinated by the mixture of cool granite and intricate oak carvings, the lovely stained glass windows, illuminated by the summer sun and the story of Jesus' crucifixion depicted in delicately crafted wooden scenes along white-washed walls. In awe I survey the interestingly decorated ceilings. My fingers glide gently over the carved ends of each pew. Whispering softly Beth is standing close to me, explaining the legend of the patron saint of this great place of worship.

I had not bargained for a guided tour of the church and the entire village but that is what Beth is giving me. Her local knowledge is quite staggering. Eventually we end up in front of my cottage again. My heart is suddenly racing. I have not felt like this in fifteen or twenty years. *You are not a teenager, Rob*, I tell myself. *Just get in the car and drive home.* "I'd really like to meet your family," Beth's voice disturbs my thoughts. "They know nothing about this - and I don't want them to," I confess. The permanent smile on Beth' pretty face disappears instantly. She is covering her mouth with one hand. "I understand," she mutters but I don't believe she does. "I must go now," I decide before my puberty-like feelings return. Beth nods and at the same time she says: "Please give me a ring if you'd like to visit again. Thanks for the lunch and the wonderful day. I've enjoyed it a lot." With that she turns away, waving but proceeding swiftly to the front door. I jump in the car and drive off, leaving the village as fast as I can.

I get home just before Angie and Melanie are being dropped off. Barbara is coming in but Charles still hasn't forgiven me so when he sees my car parked outside he resolves to stay in his. Harsh reality has caught up with me. Politely I invite Barbara to have a drink. "No, thanks, Robby. We'll be off home," she says plainly. Then she hugs my wife and leaves the house. "Did you have a nice day?" Angie asks me. "Yes, thank you," I respond. I am telling the truth here. I've had a fantastic day in fact. "I am going to have a shower if you don't mind," I tell Angie, glad to escape any further questions.

While I am upstairs my parents-in-law come back with Jordan. Our son is full of the joys of Lundy Island. He cannot stop talking about the boat trip, the bird watching with his grandad and the many seals he has seen. His face looks badly sunburnt but he seems to be very happy. Angie's parents are staying for dinner so I make sure Melanie is changed.

I am in the middle of disposing of her nappy when my mobile announces a text message. It's from Beth, telling me that I've left my tape measure behind. "I'll pick it up next time," I quickly text back. Then I delete the correspondence as usual. *Next time* - why have I chosen those words? When will next time be? With Melanie in my arms I walk downstairs. Jordan has put his photographs on my laptop having asked for permission first, of course. Everyone is admiring the pictures so we are having a peaceful evening. Angie and I are getting along fine but tonight I am quite glad to be alone in our bed. I lie awake for hours thinking about Beth. I want to see her again, sooner rather than later.

At the end of the next week the summer holiday will start which means that Jordan will be home all day. I don't know why but Angie has not seen her solicitor again, nor has she begun divorce proceedings. Jackie is having a week off so I can't go anywhere for the moment but Angie has been talking about going away. "I am not going without Dad though," Jordan insists. "Daddy has got to work, darling," Angie tries to persuade him but he does not want to hear of it. We are trying hard to work something out that suits all of us which is not easy. I am definitely prepared to go on a short family holiday – anything to get rid of my longing for Beth, anything to forget her and save my marriage.

It is Tuesday morning and I am out on a test drive with a customer when I receive a call from Beth. "I've got a problem at the cottage," she tells me. "Early this morning one of the old water pipes in the bathroom has burst leaving quite a lot of mess. A neighbour has temporarily fixed it but he reckons the whole water supply system needs changing urgently. It is going to be expensive," Beth reports. I explain that I would have to ring her back as I am not in a position to talk at present but the prospect of having to speak to her again excites me.

Unfortunately, I have to wait until I have my lunch break before I can return Beth's call. It has been a bit manic at the showroom this morning but finally I can sit back in my comfortable office chair in readiness to speak to her. "Normally I would have contacted Alan from the agency but seeing it's your property now there is no need to involve the middle-man," Beth says laughing. "I wish I could come and have a look at the problem but I can't leave here this week," I tell her. "Do you think you could get someone in to quote for the repairs, I mean, I need to know how much the job will cost me," I say. "Yes, sure. You can rely on me. The man next door thinks it will cost in the region of £3000 to £5000," Beth reports. I am gasping for air. As I don't respond Beth continues: "The work should have been done years ago. This system is very old-fashioned and worn out. The next problem will be the electrics, the man said," Beth adds. It suddenly dawns on me that I may not be able to afford to run the cottage for any length of time. I am paying off a high mortgage on our house in Launceston, and although I have a company car I've got Angie's car to run, petrol to buy, children to feed… With a deep sigh I tell Beth to obtain the quote and then ring me back.

For a couple of days I can do nothing but prepare myself for bad news. Angie is talking about a holiday abroad and I am dreaming of driving an hour down the road to see Beth. I think of her day and night, wondering how she is getting on. By the end of the week I am getting quite impatient so I ring her from work. "I've had to make enquiries in the village, Rob. A neighbour's son-in-law has a plumbing firm in Newquay and he will come and have a look at the damage tomorrow. I am OK at the moment. The emergency repairs are holding out fine for the minute," Beth reports proudly. "Thanks. I am working on finding the time and opportunity to come and see you," I reply. Immediately I am wondering if my words have sounded a little too keen. "Yes, that would be nice," Beth confirms promptly. Surely she's not as crazy about me as I am about her? I quickly dismiss those thoughts, telling myself that she is just being friendly.

When I get home that evening Jordan announces that he wants to go to "Disneyland". "What? Florida?" I ask. "No, Paris," Angie says to keep me calm. Then she adds: "Judy rang. Tom was originally taking another friend but the poor chap has gone down with chicken pox and can't go. Justin and Judy have offered to take Jordan instead." "Great - any thoughts where we and Melanie could go during that time?" I enquire. Angie shakes her head. She doesn't really want to go on holiday with me anymore.

If Justin and Judy are not going to be around for a while then I will have to come up with a different excuse why I need to go to Newquay by myself. By pure coincidence I find the ideal solution at work. I am chatting to a customer in the showroom when my eye catches a form that is lying on the table in front of us. It is the entry form for a two-day open golf tournament at Braunton in Devon. I've played in it many years ago but since I've had my family I found being away all weekend for a golf tournament a little too much. My eyes are trying to catch the closing date for entries. Fortunately my customer needs to get away urgently so he leaves me to pick up the form. The deadline is tomorrow. I will need to ring the organisers to find out if they would accept a late entry. There is absolutely nothing to lose. I can always book a room in a hotel like many of the other participants and ask Angie if she will accompany me with Melanie. As I am sure she will decline I will enter but pull out last minute. I am going to lose a bit of money but I can possibly spend two full days in Crantock without Angie knowing about it. Should she decide to come with me after all, I'll just use the room and play. At least Justin won't be there to beat me. Form in hand I walk off to get in touch with the tournament organisers at Braunton. Just as I sit down in my office I receive a text message from Beth. "Work can be done for £4800 including VAT," it reads. Where do I get that sum of money from without Angie's knowledge, I ask myself. The fairly hefty entry fee and the cost of a two night stay in the hotel at Braunton are nothing compared to that. "Thanks. Don't do anything until I arrive at the weekend – hopefully. Will ring you," I text back, and I wonder how Beth will feel about that.

I am in luck. The tournament officials are prepared to accept my entry by fax. All I need to do is send a cheque off today and find out if there is a room available anywhere once I've spoken to my wife. So far it's all working out beautifully.

As expected Angie is not keen on coming to Braunton with me. I am trying to encourage her but she says that she does not fancy hanging around all day at the hotel waiting for me to finish my rounds on the golf course and two nights with me and Melanie in one room does not appeal to her either. "You go and play, Rob. I'd rather stay here," she says. I pretend to be disappointed but at least I don't need to book a hotel room now. Excitedly I go upstairs and text Beth. "Will be with you Friday evening around 7pm," I tell her.

When you are looking forward to something the time will simply not pass. The hours and days seem to be dragging on until it is Friday. Jordan has gone off with Justin, Judy and Tom early this morning. Once home from work I am finally able to pack my own bags. As Angie is not watching I can sneak in a couple of other items apart from golfing gear. This time I am going to bring my own swimming trunks for example. To say that I am feeling excited is an understatement. With a spring in my step I carry my large golf bag to the car, push it into the boot and then I am ready to go. All I need to do now is to say good-bye to Angie and Melanie. "I wish you'd decided to come with me," I say, trying to sound ever so sincere but my wife just shrugs her shoulders. "Sorry but good luck anyway – I hope you'll win," she replies. I know very well that she no longer cares if I win or not but it does not bother me. Deep inside I sense that I am going to get the biggest prize of all – Beth.

Driving off, in strictly speaking the opposite direction, I feel strangely alive. As so often on a Friday evening there is heavy traffic. I will have to be patient and extra careful not to exceed the speed limit. The last thing I want is for the police to send a speeding fine home telling Angie that I was in Cornwall, not Devon, at the time of the offence. While a lot of my fellow golfers will be heading for Braunton this evening I am driving towards Newquay. With the car radio on at full volume I eventually enter Crantock. The teenager in me has returned with a vengeance. It is time to turn the music down and park in front of my cottage. I am not taking any luggage out of the car deliberately, just in case Beth won't let me stay the night. My tenant must have been looking out for me because the door opens immediately once I approach the cottage. "Hi, Rob. Lovely to see you," Beth greets me. She is dressed in casual shorts and a t-shirt. "I'll show you the pipes in the bathroom," she says, running up the stairs like only she can do. I follow her relatively sedately. As soon as I enter the bathroom the problem becomes apparent. The patched up pipes are looking rather dubious. There is no way I can avoid spending the money if I am going to keep the cottage. "I hope you haven't had dinner yet," Beth suddenly says. We are still in the bathroom, examining the damaged pipes. "No, I haven't actually," I reply. "Fantastic. I'm going to cook us a nice meal. How long can you stay?" Beth asks. "Two nights and two days," I respond and instantly I regret saying it so casually. Never before in just over forty years have I done anything like this. Beth is not smiling. She is fully aware of the seriousness of my response. "I'm sorry," I stutter, "I mean, yes, I ..," I try to explain helplessly, realising that I may have made a big mistake. Beth walks over to the hand-basin, her back to the slightly cracked mirror. "When I saw you for the first time, I…," she starts but she fails to complete the sentence. "What happened?" I ask, wondering if I dare touch her. "Something deep inside told me that you are going to change my life forever," she admits, looking very concerned now. "That's exactly how I felt when I first set eyes on you, once you took that awful raincoat off...," I confess softly. Beth steps forward and I take her firmly into my arms. Without any hesitation our lips meet and we kiss. The desire inside of me is causing physical pain. I have never known passion like this. Beth's skilful fingers stroke my hair, my neck. I cannot remember ever wanting anyone as much as I want her right now. Unsure if I am going too far I pull her along, out of the bathroom, towards the double bedroom. She offers no resistance whatsoever. It is not until we are lying on the bed that I ask her an important question. "Have you ever been unfaithful to your husband?" I want to know. "No, never," she confirms. In return she asks me: "Be honest, Rob – have you been cheating on your wife before?" "No, never," I reply and it is the truth. With that we undress each other and climb underneath the sheets. We are both so starved of sex that our physical union takes merely a few seconds but holding the gorgeous Beth in my arms afterwards makes me incredibly happy. "Wow," I hear her say a couple of minutes later. She is touching me so lovingly like no other woman has ever done before. "Too fast – we can do better than this," I whisper, caressing her warm breasts. "It was wonderful all the same," Beth tells me. I agree. It was the most unbelievable feeling I've ever had. We are both fulfilled and tired but still we get dressed and go downstairs. "I'm supposed to be in Braunton by now," I tell her. "Where's that?" Beth asks, starting to prepare our dinner. "Devon, near Barnstaple," I respond, watching her every move. "And what are you supposed to be doing there?" Beth wants to know. "Win," I say, chuckling. "I see," Beth comments. I feel that I owe her an explanation. "I am supposed to be playing in a golf tournament, 36 holes over two days. I am going to withdraw early tomorrow morning," I tell her. "What if your wife finds out?" Beth enquires. "She won't. She's not interested in my performance on the golf course," I reply. "Nor in your performance in bed, I guess," Beth remarks, smiling. I ignore her statement and ask her about Brian. "Does he satisfy you when he returns home from his business trips?" I ask. Beth stops what she is doing at the cooker. She turns around to face me. "Brian has got problems. He is very much older than me and he has been suffering from erectile dysfunction for some years now. We've been to see many different specialists in London. As you can imagine, money is no issue for him but our sex life has become so difficult that we have given up. I keep telling him that I don't need it, that I love him without having intercourse," Beth confesses. Then she passes me a bottle of wine and a corkscrew.

We have our dinner in the poorly furnished lounge. Our meal is simple but delicious. I am enjoying Beth's company so much that I cannot imagine being happier anywhere in the world. As it is getting dark she is lighting candles. My old cottage is quickly transformed into heaven on earth. We are in each others' arms on the old creaking sofa, we kiss and chat until we feel strong enough to make love again. Nothing and nobody can disturb us, not even the annoying sounds of our mobile phones that keep going off from time to time. We are proceeding much slower now, paying more attention to each others' needs. Beth is unbelievable. It is absolutely fantastic having sex with her. She is the most exciting woman I've ever met. Her athleticism and stamina combined with a willingness to experiment sends me into overdrive. I am just hoping that she rates my sexual prowess as highly as I rate hers. In nine and a half years of marriage nothing has even come close to this. I have no idea what the time is but the candles on the coffee table have almost completely burnt down. Beth passes me my mobile phone which has slipped into the gap between the back cushions of the well-worn old sofa. Then she gets up to fetch her own. Quietly we check our messages, voice mails and e-mails of which there are many.

I have a text from Justin, telling me that they have arrived safely in Paris and a few other, not so important, messages but there is nothing from Angie. Satisfied that I am going to get away with my secret adventure I put my mobile into alarm mode for the early morning so I won't forget to phone in with my tournament withdrawal. "Brian is coming back next week," Beth suddenly remarks. In the darkness of the room I look at her. "Is he going to come here?" I enquire. "Yes, that's his plan," Beth replies. I am yawning. "OK, let's go to bed," Beth decides. Thankfully it is almost dark outside when I leave the cottage to bring my bag in from the car. I don't want nosy neighbours to spy on me.

It has been a wise move to set the alarm on my mobile. When it goes off in the morning I am still half asleep. Beth is not even stirring. I can see the sunlight pouring through the thin bedroom curtains and I get out of bed to find the copy of my entry form. Beth wakes up as I make the important call. I am shouting as the phone signal in the old granite cottage keeps breaking up. Beth laughs at my excuses. "Severe tendonitis in the elbow!" She repeats smiling. "Wrong part of the body, sir" she comments jokingly. "Whatever, it's done now," I say happily, putting the phone away. "I'll show you where you should be hurting," Beth insists. Within seconds I am back in the bed. She is manhandling me rather unkindly but nevertheless sexily. Like animals we are starting to play-fight until Beth finally succumbs, tamed by the desire to be loved gently. We are both breathing heavily, sounding totally exhausted from our rather athletic activities. "Please, save something for later. I can't keep this up," I tell her softly. "Nonsense, Rob. You are a whole year younger than me!" she reminds me. Her sexual energy is quite amazing.

At around lunch time we are eventually getting up. Beth shows me pictures of her two sons on the computer. Brian is also in many of the photographs, of course. Naturally, I get my laptop out to show off my family, too. "You are lucky to have one of each. I would have liked to have a girl," Beth remarks sadly when she sees Jordan and Melanie. *It's not too late,* I think to myself but fortunately I am not saying it aloud.

We go downstairs to have breakfast, lunch or whatever it is now. To our dismay the sun has disappeared behind dark clouds. "I would normally have gone for a swim this morning but it's very windy. Let's give it a miss," Beth decides, looking dreamily out of the window. "We'll go for a walk instead," I suggest as I am in need of fresh air after so much sex. We take a shower and get ready to go out. "No holding hands or kissing until we reach the cliff path," Beth instructs me. I understand and obey. At a fast pace we approach the beach. "Wouldn't you rather be playing golf?" Beth wants to know. "No," I reply truthfully. Although the weather is dull and the summer breeze quite cool there is absolutely nowhere I'd rather be right now. I can't wait until we reach the safety of the coast path where I am allowed to take Beth's hand. We walk along quietly for a while until the subject of the water supply repairs raises its ugly head again. "I have to be honest, Beth. Finding almost £5000 - and without Angie knowing about it - is impossible," I say. "Yes, I can imagine that it must be difficult. It's much easier for me. I can make that kind of sum available very easily – or, even better, if you would be prepared to sell the property to us, I will persuade Brian to buy it before the repairs are being carried out. He will want to do a lot of modernisation work anyway," Beth proposes. I can sense that she is keen on leaving me with little option. Suddenly she stops walking. "You must realise that this cannot go on forever. If you divorce your wife the courts will find out about the property anyway and even if you stay with her she has a right to know," she tells me. "But if I sell to you and Brian …," I start but I am not really sure what I am trying to explain. Beth puts her warm arms around me. Then we kiss, long and passionately. I don't want to think about the cottage, not right now.

The tide has receded so far that the vast beach has more than doubled in size. "I am going to show you something special," Beth says eagerly. Her words make me smile. She has already shown me enough "special things" over the last few hours. I don't know if I can take any more. Suddenly she stops in her tracks again, holding on to my arm. We are at the top of the beach, just below the high dunes. A strong sea breeze is driving fine white sand into our eyes. "Look at those high cliffs over there," Beth says, pointing at a long steep wall of solid dark rock in the distance. "Those are the cliffs of West Pentire. There are many caves and inlets in those rocks. It is dangerous to go over there when the tide is coming in but now is the time to visit. I will show you a particular place, a cave that contains a carving and some lovely words." With that Beth walks on, pulling me along with her. We are on our way from the deep sandy area to the more rocky part of the enormous beach. Beth knows exactly where she is going. She soon makes us jump over large pools and long channels of clear sea water until we reach the famous cave.

Beth's knowledge of the beach is impressive, and she can also recite the story that locals tell about this amazing spot with its distinctive carving of a woman's face and a small horse. The words on that solid, flat, shiny and wet rock read:

Mar not my face but let me be,
Secure in this lone cavern by the sea,
Let the wild waves around me roar,
Kissing my lips for evermore

"It is said that a woman rode her horse along this beach one day. She did not notice that the tide was fast approaching. Both rider and horse drowned here. The lady's heartbroken lover carved her image and the words into this rock to remember her," Beth tells me. With that her small hands are beginning to stroke the smooth wet surface of the rock, just like they have touched me earlier today. "Beautiful, don't you think?" she asks softly. I stand back, my trainers rapidly soaking up water in that rocky cave. Silently I nod but deep down I find this place a little spooky.

As I turn around I cannot help looking out to sea. It is not hard to imagine that this legend may well be true. The tide seems miles out now but I can picture this beach in the winter when the ocean becomes more unpredictable, when massive waves crash in, hitting those rocks with enormous power... The thought alone make me want to leave – and fast.

I take Beth's wet hand, dragging her away from this special cave. My socks feel sodden now and I cannot wait to take them off.

Barefoot we walk on in silence as large drops of rain start falling. "Come on, quick. Let's go home," Beth encourages me. She makes me jog all the way back to the other side of the beach. It's a good job that I am reasonably fit. I can think of many men who wouldn't be able to keep up with her. Due to our surprising speed we arrive back at the cottage without getting too wet. While I am brushing layers of sticky sand off our footwear and dry my feet Beth offers to make us a few sandwiches. We are also starting a serious discussion about the future. "Have you ever thought of leaving Brian, considering all you've told me?" I ask. "No, never. I know it must sound strange to you but I do love him, in a way. We've been married for 20 years and the thought of a separation has not once crossed my mind. In the beginning everything was fine. Brian was the love of my life, I really mean that. For someone so wealthy he is very genuine, incredibly kind and I believe one hundred percent faithful. Although he has never been around a lot he is a great father. He has helped to develop my dream career so I can now do what I love most – writing. All I've ever wanted he has done for me. I'm not ungrateful. Until you came along I was quite content without sex. I was satisfied writing about it in my books," Beth answers. I nod but I am not sure if I can follow her line of thinking.

Nervously I play with my wedding ring. "I've never thought my marriage could ever fail either," I confess. "I hate the thought of splitting up," I add. Beth passes me a plate full of food. "Frankly, I hate the thought of having an affair," she says. Taking a deep breath she explains: "Once you leave here tomorrow I will be longing for you every minute of the day. It will be unbearable and even more so when facing Brian after all this. You know what will happen – we will both be scheming for the slightest window of opportunity. It's dangerous. It would break Brian's heart if he ever found out. He is feeling inadequate as a husband. I must not hurt him, ever." Beth's strong words make me ponder. Should I offer to leave tonight and promise never to return? Suddenly a warm smile appears on her gorgeous face. "How about going for a drive in a minute?" she suggests. "Yes, OK," I respond, rather lamely.

Half an hour later we sit in her car, a swish black Mercedes coupe, heading for the coast road. The rain has stopped but it's not a brilliant day. Beth takes me to West Pentire to show me another famous beach. This one is called Polly Joke. We have to leave the car in the official car park and walk down to the water. I am surprised to see a second stunningly beautiful sandy cove. "Well, I have to say, you know so much about this area. You could become a travel adviser!" I tell her. "I spend quite a lot of time driving around Cornwall," Beth informs me. "When I need inspiration for my books I visit places that I can use for my stories. It's fun," she explains. I have to admit that I have become quite familiar with the area around Launceston, mainly due to hundreds of test drives with customers, and I know most of the golf courses in Cornwall but not too much else. Angie is Cornish born and bred but I have only lived here permanently for three years, since I packed up travelling the professional golfing circuit and starting the job at the car dealership.

Beth is in her element. She cannot wait to take me along other interesting parts of the Cornish coast line, down steep lanes, through narrow roads and even across vast expanses of sand. Occasionally we park up and walk for a while, hand in hand, kissing and cuddling. "Tell me more about yourself, please," Beth encourages me as we walk along the coast path. So I tell her about my work, my past, Justin and Judy, my colleagues and neighbours but at the end of it all the conversation reverts to Angie and my children. In return I hear a lot about Philip and Darren, Beth's two sons, about her success as an author, about her ambitious publisher, her pride in her sporting achievements and her home in Surrey, about cars, holidays and, of course, Brian.

As the hours pass the sun is making one short appearance but it is too late for anything else but the return to Crantock. Sitting next to Beth in the car I am suddenly beginnng to worry about tomorrow. I don't want this new relationship to end and nor does she. Full of sorrow I look at the magical scenery as we ride along. Beth is strangely quiet, too. I can sense that she must have similar thoughts. We enter the village and slowly approach the cottage. Once Beth has parked her car she says: "Whatever happens, Rob, I will never forget this. Last night and today have been the most wonderful experiences of my entire life," she whispers before kissing me passionately. I say nothing. I have fallen in love.

Having made a conscious decision not to visit any bars, pubs or restaurants together this evening, just in case someone may recognise us, we decide to cook our own dinner. Looking out of the road-side window we can see that Crantock has come to life tonight. The small village seems to be buzzing with people in the streets. "There must be something special on," Beth reckons. Standing close to her I sense that she would love to go out and have fun but it is sensible to keep our relationship secret and not mix with the locals. "I expect Alan has told you that there is no central heating here. If you want to update this place you'll need a decent heating system," Beth remarks suddenly. She walks over to the open fire place, kneels in front of it and carefully arranges kindling wood and sheets of newspaper before setting the small heap alight. "Brian was in the Scouts. He's taught me how to do this," she explains proudly when I admire her practical skills.

It is my turn to prepare food in the tiny kitchen. I don't think that I am a particularly good chef but I do know how to feed myself, my family and friends. The atmosphere in the cottage is extremely cosy tonight. Beth has gone upstairs to e-mail her sons and Brian, leaving me alone for a few minutes to gather my thoughts. All of a sudden I feel quite emotional. I am afraid of the future, I am scared, petrified. What have I done? How am I going to cope with life after this? I am again thinking about tomorrow, having to leave all this behind, return to reality. For a moment I feel almost sick but then Beth comes down the stairs. "Hm, smells lovely," she remarks, smiling. Not commenting I pass her a glass of wine. "Cheers," I say quickly, desperate to forget what has just gone through my troubled mind. A few minutes later we are sitting in front of the fire eating our dinner. "What time will you have to leave tomorrow?" Beth asks me. It seems that she can read me like a book. "Sometime in the afternoon," I respond slowly.

Beth is trying her utmost to distract me from feeling sad but when we eventually go to bed we find it difficult to fully relax. We cuddle and talk for hours. At one stage I am starting to wonder whether I will be able to satisfy her tonight but then it happens naturally. It is so different this time. Whereas we were lusting for each other yesterday we are making love tonight. Something has created a deep emotional bond between us which makes the thought that this may well be last time an awful lot harder.

As we wake up in the morning Beth tells me that she now believes in love at first sight. She says that she fell in love with me the day she showed me around the cottage. Then she pushes me out of bed, insisting that we must go for a swim today. I am feeling totally exhausted, mentally and physically, but I can't let her down. We walk to the beach which is still virtually deserted on this relatively cool Sunday morning and take a dip.

After lunch I have to prepare myself for going home. It's tough, really hard. To think that I may not see Beth again for several weeks, to think that when I see her the next time I may well have to pretend that nothing ever happened between us, to think that I may never be allowed to sleep with her again, to think that we may never be able to repeat this wonderful weekend, to think that I may not be able to talk to her, kiss her, play with her. It's breaking my heart. I'm not made for a one or two night stand, I get too involved emotionally.

Beth is crying which doesn't help at all. She's in my arms, weeping. It's the same for her, maybe worse. At this moment in time I can't even kiss her. I am just holding her, squeezing her, don't want to let her go. "I love you, Rob, love you like I've never loved anyone before. When you walked in here that day, just before Alan arrived, I knew you were the one, after all these years, after all I've ever felt and still feel for Brian," she whispers. Then she wriggles herself out of my arms. She walks across the room, goes to the old wooden cupboard and pulls a little box out. "I would have loved to give you one of my books but it's too dangerous. I'd like you to have something to remember me by, in case we can never be together again," she solemnly declares. In front of me she opens the box and out comes a ring, a magnificent golden ring with three small colourful stones set in a kind of triangle. "Keep this safe somewhere. It's only small. Keep it a secret but close to you at all times and think of me. Maybe one day, when your daughter is older, and we've got over our affair, you may give it to her. It's always been my lucky charm and it will be yours," she says sincerely.

I don't know what to say but nevertheless I take the ring, kiss it and take it out to my car. With Beth following and watching me I open the boot, pull my golf bag forward, without taking it out completely, and let the ring disappear in one of the bag's large side pockets. "It'll be safe in there," I confirm, wondering what I can give her in return. My fingers search in another pocket of my heavy bag. "Here, this is a special ball marker. It was given to me by a famous Scottish golfer when I was a junior. He told me that I would be a professional golfer one day and he was right. This marker is very dear to me. I have used it for tournaments ever since. You can imagine what it means to me," I say, handing it to Beth. "Thank you, I will treasure it, you know I will," she replies, still tearful, her small hand closing firmly around the coin-like item. We cannot possibly stay out here, in front of the cottage, any longer. The neighbours may see us or overhear our conversation. So we quickly say our last good-byes and I drive off, heart-broken, exhausted, tired and inconsolable.

I get as far as the main road but then I have to stop. Like a man possessed I brake hard to pull into a lay-by. I am choking, struggling to contain myself. It is all my fault and I know it. How can I face Angie in an hour's time, pretending nothing has happened, telling her blatant lies? What I have done is unforgiveable. I lean back in the driver's seat and close my eyes. There is no way out. I must drive home.

As I approach Launceston the afternoon sun has pushed the dark clouds away. It is quite pleasant outside now. Nervously I turn into our road, park the car in front of our house and take a deep breath. Angie and Melanie are in the garden. "Oh, hi, I didn't hear you arrive," Angie greets me. She does not get up from her easy chair. Melanie is playing with large plastic bricks. Instantly she looks up and says: "Dada, dada," which no doubt means "hello, Daddy". I bend down to pick her up and take her into my arms. "How did you get on?" Angie enquires. "Not good, didn't play well at all," I lie. Before Angie can ask any more questions I carry my daughter into the house. I feel terrible but I must stay calm, play my game.

So far everything is going fine. I unload my bag from the car and Angie makes us a cup of tea. "You look tired," she remarks, assessing me in a way that makes me feel uncomfortable. "I am," I reply and that is actually the truth. I am totally exhausted indeed but I dare not admit that. "Jordan has rung from Paris," my wife tells me then. "Seems like they are having a brilliant time," she adds. "That's great," I respond. Sitting here with Angie is absolute torture. She could be asking me an awkward question at any time. I am so afraid that I will not be able to give the correct answer. This must never happen again. I am no good at this, just can't do it. Having an affair is not for me. It's too nerve-wrecking. I am already wishing I could sink to my knees, hide in shame and confess my sins – but I can't. I can't hurt Angie like this, not now, not yet, if ever.

The evening drags on. Angie, Melanie and I are having dinner, just a light one but an evening meal all the same. I put my daughter to bed to give Angie a break and then I return downstairs.

"I've been thinking while you were away, Rob. Barbara has asked me the other day if we were prepared to visit a marriage counsellor, talk to someone about our problems who may be able to help sorting them out. Occasionally couples find a solution and even get back together again. Personally, I believe it's a good idea and I would like to try it," she says. "I don't," I protest immediately. "I have no intention for us to split up anyway – so what's the point? It's you who thinks it's all over, not me. I've been trying hard to make our marriage work. I don't want to speak to anyone else about my private problems. If there is anything to talk about you and I can talk here, now. We don't need a counsellor!" I continue and I am getting quite worked up, more than I would normally do. Angrily I lean back into the sofa. I don't agree with involving a Third Party. Why can't we talk about our differences here at home? "Go on, tell me straight - what is your biggest concern? Where am I going wrong? Is it that I am out of the house too much? Is it that I am a bad father? Is it that I'd like you to sleep with me? What is it? Tell me, what's your problem?" My nerves are not holding out well at all. I am shouting, getting a little out of control. Angie shakes her head. "Can't you see it, Rob? You are losing it again. I don't trust you anymore and we no longer have a loving relationship," she says. I am starting to get worried. She does not trust me. I hope and pray that she has not found out about my withdrawal from the tournament. Trust is a big issue… "I'd just like you to think about it, in your own time. You don't have to make a decision right now," Angie suggests calmly. With that she goes upstairs to bed and I am left alone.

When I am in bed I am very tempted to text Beth but I decide not to. I don't want to stir up the memories, make it difficult for her or myself. I am so tired that I fall asleep almost instantaneously.

At work the next day Jackie catches me yawning and looking a little sorry for myself. "'you alright, Rob?" she asks me. I nod silently but she has known me long enough to realise that I am unhappy. As it is still very quiet in the showroom she takes a seat in my visitor's chair. "I have a feeling that you are leaving us to get away from something. Am I right?" she enquires. Jackie has always been my confidante, from day one. I have learned so much from her since I first started to work here, and in return I taught her what I know about engines and the technical side of the job. We have always got on well. She is the best colleague anyone could wish for. "Angie wants a divorce," I admit lamely. "I see," Jackie responds calmly. "But I don't, I really don't. I don't want to get divorced," I emphasize now, and my voice is getting louder. Luckily my telephone rings and brings an end to my embarrassing outburst. Jackie rises from the chair and leaves my office. Perhaps I owe her an apology, a proper explanation but the prospect of selling one more car before I take up my new post calms me down instantly.

Strangely enough I am having a fantastic day as far as work is concerned. I have taken an order for a brand new car and sold one of our previously-owned VWs from the firm's forecourt. "Pity that you are leaving," our boss says to me as we are closing up after the last potential customer has left the dealership. Jackie is nowhere to be seen. I would have liked to take her out for a quick drink to explain myself but she must have gone home early.

Up to Tuesday evening I am getting away with my secrets of the weekend but when I arrive at our house after work there is a nasty surprise waiting for me. Barbara is sitting in our kitchen, next to Angie, and they have Barbara's laptop on the table in front of them. As I enter the room Barbara turns the computer around and shows me the starter's list for Braunton. She points at a red line in the middle of the screen: Robert Cunningham - withdrawn. Both women look at me with thunderous expressions.

"So if you didn't play, where have you been?" Angie asks. I am numb, lost for words. "You said you didn't play very well but it seems that you did not play at all. You are lying, aren't you? I can find out if you ever turned up at Braunton. I doubt it somehow. So where have you been?"

Angie is beside herself with anger. I drop into the sofa. Game over - I have to come clean or let's say cleaner. I'll never get away with any further lies. Angie keeps on accusing me of being a liar, she swears at me, tells me that she will never be able to trust me again. This goes on for ten minutes until I say: "Hang on, Ange. I'll tell you where I've been. I should have told you before." With that I get up, go to my briefcase and pull the solicitor's letter out. Silently I pass it to her to read. Barbara realises that it time for her to leave so she packs up her laptop, hugs Angie quickly and rushes out of our home.

"I don't understand," Angie comments when she has read the letter. "I wanted to have a look at the property alone before telling you about it. There are tenants in the cottage. This weekend was the only time I could see it. That's why I withdrew from Braunton," I try and explain the awkward situation. I know I am not making much sense but it's all I can do in the circumstances. Angie hands the letter back to me. "According to the date of the letter you've known about this for ages and you kept it a secret – why? Why didn't you want me to know?" she asks me. I have no answer. "This is where our problem lies, Rob. You keep doing things behind my back. In the past we used to tell each other everything but it has all changed. We are drifting apart, more and more," Angie says. She looks terribly sad now. "The news of my inheritance came as a bit of a shock, to be honest. I had absolutely no idea that my aunt would leave me anything. I never had anything to do with her and I did not even know that she had died. I needed to see the place to believe it," I stutter slowly. "But why not with me, with us? Why couldn't we all go and see it?" Angie enquires. This time it is me who is shaking my head. "I don't know. I want you to come next time though," I say firmly. "I still don't understand why it took you all weekend to see one cottage. It really doesn't make sense," Angie continues. "There was a lot to sort out with the letting agent and the current tenants. We can't afford to keep it. It will have to be sold," I reply. "I see. You've made that decision already – all without talking to me about it, showing it to me, discussing it with me. Why? Why does my opinion not count anymore? If you call this a marriage – I don't," Angie shouts at me.

At least she has not kicked me out. She is upset, furious with me but she simply goes to Melanie's room and that's it. I am heaving a sigh of relief but I know that this may well be the final straw. So far she is not aware that there is so much more to this story but where we are now is bad enough.

Working out my notice also means more freedom as far as time off is concerned. I am due a couple of days holiday and on Thursday morning I suggest to Angie that we should make a trip to Crantock before Jordan comes back on Friday. I have shown Angie some pictures that I have taken on my mobile phone and somehow they seem to have sparked something off in her. She is reluctant at first but then she agrees with me that it would be better if we went to Crantock without Jordan.

After breakfast I put on my best acting skills. My heart beating like a drum I make a call to Beth's mobile. "Good morning, is that Mrs Henderson?" I ask politely. Beth understands the situation immediately. "Yes, speaking," she replies formally but I sense that she has already recognised both my number and my voice. I ask her whether it would be convenient if my wife, my little daughter and I could come and have a look at the cottage today. "Yes, certainly. Just let me check with my husband," Beth replies. I am relieved to think that Brian is around as well. Beth gives us the go-ahead for this afternoon. She tells me that she and her husband may be on the beach later so she will leave the key under a flower pot for us.

On the way to Crantock I talk to Angie about the village, my impressions of the cottage, the issues that I've discussed with the letting agent and I also briefly mention the Hendersons. Melanie has gone to sleep in the back of the car so we have quite a pleasant journey.

With the weather being warm and sunny I expect that Beth and Brian will be on the beach which is a great relief.

Although I am longing to see Beth again I think it is best if I don't set eyes on her. It will make the visit so much easier.

Despite being Cornish Angie says that she has never been to Crantock before. As I drive into the village, past the post office and shop, the memorial hall and the tiny village green towards the beach she is expressing her delight: "What a quaint little place!" she says instantly. Slowly I am approaching the cottage and I notice that the space that I've used for parking has now been taken up by a large silver Mercedes which is no doubt Brian's. There is not too much room left but I squeeze my modest VW behind it. Angie is really excited. "Wow, it's lovely!" she exclaims. I am surprised that she likes the look of the old cottage but it appears that Beth has done some work in the front garden and in the sunshine it looks quite presentable.

Carrying the sleeping Melanie in my arms I lead Angie to the front door. "Just knock. If no one answers the Hendersons will be on the beach," I tell her. In the meantime I am trying to establish which flower pot covers the key. As there is nobody home we search for it and eventually find it in the back garden. Again, Beth has tidied the flower beds up considerably. She must have spent hours weeding. Everything is looking neat. Angie is genuinely impressed. "Come on then, I'll show you the interior," I say and unlock my property.

Having known my wife for more than ten years I cannot believe that she is so taken with the place. I've always thought she liked more modern houses. "What a cosy little cottage! Bit old-fashioned but very cute," Angie exclaims excitedly.

Melanie has woken up and she looks absolutely mesmerised. "Look where we are, darling. Do you like it?" I ask my daughter but she cannot care less. She is struggling in my arms, wanting to go down and walk. Luckily Angie takes over. I lead mother and daughter into the bathroom to show Angie the damaged pipes. "The agent says it'll cost nearly £5000 to repair this. The cottage needs a completely new water system – and central heating," I report. Angie does not listen. She has left the bathroom and is moving on into the master bedroom. I watch her pacing up and down, taking rough measurements, inspecting window frames, touching walls, checking the ceiling. She is taking such an interest in the property that it frightens me. "Don't sell it, Rob. It's got potential. I'd love to take this project on. If we do it up during the winter it will be ready for lettings again in the summer. All the work will pay for itself," Angie enthuses. "We," I point out sharply. In my mind I have flashbacks of my weekend with Beth. I'd rather sell than being reminded of it all of the time.

I have no idea how long we spend viewing the property but suddenly I hear voices. Although it is warm in the cottage I begin to freeze. "Hello, anyone home?" Beth shouts up the stairs. Angie and I must have left the front door open. "Yes, we are upstairs," I reply confidently, trying hard not to sound nervous. Melanie is getting bored, pulling her mother towards the stairs. Before we can come down Beth has reached the top. "Hi, you must be Mrs Cunningham," she says, facing Angie. "Please call me Angie. Nice to meet you," my wife replies, offering Beth her hand. "I'm Beth. My husband and I have rented the cottage until 31st August," Beth quickly explains. She hardly

acknowledges me and I don't blame her. Angie introduces
Melanie who has had enough. She is crying now.

We go downstairs where we meet Brian. He is tall and
slim. His silvery grey hair reminds me of certain
distinguished gentlemen I have met at golf clubs around the
country. Brian is one of those types - very classy, almost
elegant, in his good-quality polo shirt and long shorts. Beth
offers to make us a cup of tea which Angie accepts
immediately. I feel terrible to say the least. On top of it all
Melanie is misbehaving. She is having tantrums which I find
really embarrassing. "Hey, young lady. I tell you what: You
and I will go out into the garden and I will show you
something," Brian says to her. With that he picks Melanie up
and walks off. I keep close on his heels in case my daughter
plays up but to my great surprise she is calming down. As
we arrive in the back garden Brian points to a beautiful cast-
iron weather vane. "I bought it in the local shop this
morning. If you live by the seaside you will need to know
which direction the wind is coming from," he explains to
Melanie. While my daughter is fascinated, I am getting
uncomfortable in my own skin. Brian lets Melanie touch the
skilfully crafted black cockerel. Then he turns to me. "My
wife tells me that you are going to sell," he says. I shrug my
shoulders. "I don't know. I will have to discuss it with my
wife first," I respond hesitantly. "Well, I'd like to make you
an offer," he continues. I can see that he is serious. He is
dangling a large carrot in front of me and I am tempted to
grab it but last minute I back out. "As I said I am keeping
my options open at the moment," I stress. Then I take my
daughter from him and walk back to the house.

Inside I can hear Angie and Beth laughing. They seem to be getting on fine. Once I am in ear-shot I can listen to their conversation. Angie is telling Beth what she will be doing to the cottage during the winter, making quite clear that she has no intention of selling it. As I approach the small kitchen Beth turns around. She is wearing a short sexy beach dress and flip-flops. Smiling she passes me my tea, in the same colourful mug that she used to give me last weekend. Then she goes to the old kitchen cupboard and searches for biscuits. Melanie is most grateful that she eventually finds them.

Since I have temporarily rejected Brian's idea of an offer he ignores me. There is a strange kind of tension building up between us. I am glad that Angie does not seem to notice it. She is chatting happily to Beth, leaving me in charge of Melanie. All I want is go home now. Having to look at the pretty Beth but not being allowed to touch her drives me crazy. Besides I am not too keen on her husband.

"We have taken up by far too much of your time. After all, you are on holiday," I say to Brian. "Oh, that's no problem. It was nice having you around," Beth says before her husband can answer. "Yes, Rob is right. We must leave. It was very kind of you to let us have a look around again today, considering that my husband has spent so much time here already when you should be enjoying your holidays," Angie responds apologetically. "It's a pleasure, honestly," Beth says. Thankfully she is avoiding eye contact with me.

A couple of minutes later we are back in the car. "Nice couple, the Hendersons. If we get holiday makers like them all of the time we will be laughing all the way to the bank," Angie says smiling. I start the car and decide to drive down to the two large car parks near the beach. "We could have walked down here," Angie complains when I hand over money to the young car park attendant at the upper car park. "It wasn't convenient to leave the car where I parked it," I insist. I am so relieved to be away from the Hendersons but, of course, I cannot explain it to my wife. Angie, Melanie and I get out and I show my girls the beach. On a day like today the vast beach looks fabulous. As the tide is in, the river Gannel and the luxury properties in the hillside along its banks look even more impressive than usual. "It's beautiful here, Rob. If at all possible you must keep the cottage. We'll find the money for the repairs somehow," Angie says enthusiastically, taking her sandals off. We walk silently through the warm soft sand before I make my way to the ice-cream kiosk to satisfy my little daughter. In the light summer breeze we spend an hour walking along the beach, allowing Melanie to go for a paddle. This is the ideal opportunity to take my wife's hand, in an effort to mend our broken relationship, and to talk about the future but here and now where the memories of last weekend are so vivid, so fresh in my mind I cannot bring myself to do it. Angie strolls along next to me, seemingly happy but she does not touch me. We are just friends, not lovers.

On the way home we stop at a road-side pub to have a meal. "It'll be different at home once Jordan is back," Angie remarks as we sit down in the evening sunshine. I nod absent-mindedly. It is certainly a lot more difficult to hide our problems from a bright eight-year-old. Angie is smiling confidently. "Once the Hendersons have moved out you must cancel the contract with the letting agent. We don't need to pay him when I can take over the administration of the cottage. You'll be busy with your new job in Plymouth and it will give me something useful to do," she tells me. Her words surprise me. "What about our separation?" I ask. "I don't know," Angie responds slowly. Her face looks sad again all of a sudden. "We can't carry on like this – with you on the guest bed in Melanie's room and the hostile atmosphere in our home," I say, trying to gauge my wife's reaction.

Life is so unfair. The way I am feeling at the moment is that I would like to sell the cottage, pay off the mortgage on our house and forget all about it but Angie has fallen in love with the place and wants to keep it. I can see another huge argument brewing on the horizon. Perhaps we are no longer compatible. While I am drinking my half, Angie is jotting down thoughts for alterations, repairs and renewals. Melanie is sitting in the highchair next to me playing with a beer mat. My mind is wandering. Even if I did separate from Angie would I be able to see Beth ever again? If I don't sell the cottage to Brian she will spend most of her time in Surrey and then there will be her sons to consider as well. Even if her husband is away quite often it may not be practical to meet up. I wish I could get last weekend out of my head.

The next day Jordan arrives home just after I've returned from work. Within seconds we have a house full - Tom and Jordan, Justin and Judy, Angie, Melanie and me. Everyone seems very relaxed and happy. "We had a super time, Dad.

It was so cool!" Jordan enthuses while hugging me wildly. "I look forward to hearing all about it," Angie says before inviting Justin and Judy to stay for a bite to eat and some drinks.

We are having quite a pleasant evening until my mobile goes off. "Rob, it's Brian Henderson," a male voice greets me. I step outside onto our patio to take the call. "Hi, Brian. What can I do for you?" I enquire, trying to sound cheerful. "The water pipe has gone again, I am afraid. We don't have any water now. I must insist that you get it fixed immediately," Brian requests. Nervously I check my watch. "I know you have not been the owner of the cottage for long but the pipe damage should have been repaired straight away. My wife says she has been managing with the emergency repairs for days. That's unacceptable, Rob. You are responsible for the cottage," Brian continues. "I'll see what I can do. I'll ring you back," I agree reluctantly. Swearing I put my mobile back into my pocket.

Unsure how to proceed I return to my family and friends. "What's up?" Angie wants to know. She can guess from the expression on my face that I have just received bad news. I signal to Justin to follow me outside. "It's the cottage…," I say and then I begin to explain the situation. "I'll help you find a plumber in Newquay," Justin offers immediately. He's outside, searching the internet on his fancy i-phone and makes several calls. Armed with pen and paper I am standing by his side, writing down names, telephone numbers and addresses. It is not easy calling anyone out on a Friday evening but we don't give up. I don't think I have ever been so grateful for Justin's friendship. My so-called "best mate" has rarely been as valuable as tonight. In less than an hour he has managed to instruct a Newquay-based firm which is prepared to visit the Hendersons and fix the water supply. "It'll cost you though....," Justin remarks drily.

While the boys are playing happily the ladies are getting quite concerned about us. Angie has been waiting to serve the food. Before I can sit down I have to ring Brian back. As I expected he is not particularly friendly towards me but I think he does appreciate my efforts. Reasonably satisfied, and mightily relieved, I join my family and friends at the dinner table. Anyone watching us all together this evening would never believe that Angie and I are considering a divorce.

Unfortunately Justin, Judy and Tom have to leave shortly after dinner. It's been a long day for them and they still have to drive several miles to get back to their home near Bodmin. I can see that Jordan is absolutely shattered and needs to go to bed. To be honest, I feel the same but I offer my wife to help her with the dishes. "Don't worry about them tonight, I'll do them in the morning," she rejects me which is a shame as we could have had a private conversation in the kitchen. Shrugging my shoulders I go upstairs, large figures spinning around in my head. In the next few days I can expect to receive a hefty bill for the special call-out, and as the system needs replacing badly, I can definitely add on nearly £5000. This will have to come out of our savings, hard earned cash put back for holidays, the children's education, a future new car for Angie or whatever. We cannot just put all our money into the cottage. If I sell, I won't have any further worries. I must put my foot down.

Once in bed I am thinking of Beth. If I sell to Brian she will spend many weeks of the year working in Cornwall, giving us a much better chance of meeting again. I know it's selfish but if my marriage is over I'd like a little bit of happiness elsewhere.

Angie, Melanie and Jordan are still asleep when I leave the house for work the next morning. I am busy until about 11am but then I feel obliged to make a call to the Hendersons to find out how the plumber got on last night. Brian answers the phone immediately. "When your people eventually came they could not do much for us. We are still without water this morning. The leak has again been patched up and the firm is going to send someone else later today who will renew the whole system. This incident has spoilt our holiday and I shall be deducting a fair sum of money from the rental cost," Brian tells me in no uncertain terms. Apart from "sorry" there is not much I can say. I am hoping that this is the end of the call but Brian suddenly reminds me: "Listen, I am still prepared to take that cottage off your hands. Considering that you are going to bear the cost for the new water supply I am going to up my offer slightly. You would be a fool to turn me down." There and then he makes me a fantastic new offer. It sounds incredibly attractive. I have to swallow hard and force myself not to accept it on the spot. "I'll think about it," I mutter uneasily. "Don't take too long. I will be leaving for Brussels on Wednesday and I may not be able to travel back to Cornwall for some time. If you'd like to meet me for a discussion it'll have to be very soon," he responds quickly.

Frowning I look at my phone which has suddenly gone dead. I hate being pushed into a corner. Who does Brian

Henderson think he is? How can I possibly make up my mind in the next two or three days? The call has completely thrown me. For a minute I feel dazed, like having been hit with a hammer. I must carry a pained expression on my face because my next customer is getting quite concerned about me until I eventually manage a wry smile. "I'm fine, really," I say a little unconvincingly and then I finally get on with my day's work again.

On my way home later in the afternoon I am considering discussing the situation with Angie. I know very well what her answer will be but I realise that I have kept too many important issues from her lately. Determined to improve our failing relationship I park my car, ready for a serious conversation. Entering the house I find that it is absolutely quiet inside. There is a note on the kitchen table advising me that Angie has taken Jordan and Melanie to see Barbara and Charles' daughters compete in a riding competition. My wife has left no indication when they will return. Partly relieved but also disappointed I drop into our lovely soft sofa. I would like to talk to someone, most of all to Beth which is of course impossible while Brian is around. Initially I just sit here, weighing up the options but then I phone Justin.

He's had the day off and he is sounding totally relaxed. "There are a couple of interesting tournaments coming up soon. You and I should enter. We haven't...," he starts but I won't let him finish. "Hang on, Justin. I've got more pressing matters on my mind than playing golf with you!" I snap at him. This takes the wind out of his sails immediately. "Sorry but Jude and I were under the impression that you and Angie were getting back on track. What's up now?" he enquires. "It's all very complicated but basically I want to sell the cottage," I tell him. "Why? You've only just taken possession. I thought...," Once again I am interrupting my good friend. "I've had an offer, Justin, a really great offer. I know Angie doesn't agree but I'll never get this opportunity again. It's too good to miss. It's my inheritance, my cottage but I feel that if I am going ahead it will definitely be the end of my marriage. I don't know what to do anymore," I moan.

For a few seconds there is silence on the other end of the line. "Hang tight for a bit. What's the rush? If whoever made you that offer seriously wants the cottage they can wait, can't they? You never know, by letting them stew you may even get a better price still," Justin advises eventually. What do they say? Still waters run deep. That Justin is a tough cookie, if he wants to be. I wish I had his nerve. "You may well be right but I just can't stand the hassle anymore. Angie wants this, I want that. We can't agree on anything anymore. This house is not a happy place at the moment. At least if I don't have to worry about the cottage any longer we can concentrate on each other again, I don't know...," I reply, feeling and sounding very confused. "Is that what you really want, Rob?" Justin suddenly asks. "Up to now it was, yes, but I'm not so sure anymore," I confess sadly. "Right, in that case have you considered trying to separate from Angie, I mean, move out for a while to see how it goes?" Justin suggests. I shake my head but of course Justin can't see that. I have to think about my response. "Move to Plymouth. That's where you'll have to be in a few weeks' time anyway. It's not too far away for you to see your kids but far enough to have a bit of space. Give it a go. You'll either come to the conclusion that you can't exist without Angie or you will find that there is life in the old dog yet. Come on, Robby. I hate to see you in this state," Justin continues.

The phone wedged between my face and my shoulder I get up and walk to the kitchen to fetch a beer. "It's a big step," I remark slowly. "It only seems like it to you now but once you experience total freedom you will find it OK," Justin encourages me. He doesn't know that I have already tasted a new life. Maybe that's why I find it so difficult to handle the present situation.

I am glad that this conversation is coming to an abrupt end as I can hear the key being turned in the door. My family has finally returned. Melanie is sleeping in her mother's arms and Jordan won't speak to me but I don't know why. Angie's face looks pale and tired. "Hi, doesn't look as if you had a good day," I greet my wife carefully. She simply shrugs her shoulders and takes Melanie upstairs. Jordan has already sped up to his room without acknowledging me. To be honest I have rarely felt as uncomfortable in my own home as I do tonight. I open a second bottle of beer but somehow I have lost my enthusiasm for a Saturday night drink.

At breakfast the next morning I announce that I will be moving out. Having thought about it all night long I have come to the conclusion that Justin is right. I have to do something about this miserable domestic situation. Angie is taking the news much better than I expected. It's only Jordan who breaks down and cries. That is the hardest thing to bear. I hate myself so much for hurting the children. What is happening here is not their fault.

As I am packing my belongings I feel as low as I've ever felt in my entire life. I am not proud of leaving my wife and two lovely children. In silence I get on with throwing my clothes into a large suitcase. Nobody wants to see me or talk to me. They let me get on until I am ready for the off. "I'll be in touch with details where you can contact me," I promise Angie. She nods but she does not look upset. Jordan has locked himself into his room so I let him be. I kiss Melanie's warm little forehead like I usually do when I go to work. Then I must leave the house before I change my mind or break down in tears. I jump into my car. Like a man possessed I turn the key, rev the engine and rush down the road. This whole situation feels unreal, distressing. Eventually, about half way to Plymouth, I stop by the roadside to ring Brian Henderson. "I'd like to discuss your offer," I tell him as calmly as I can. Brian is absolutely delighted. "Great, whenever it suits you," he says. "I can meet you this evening if that's convenient," I propose. Within seconds we have agreed on 7pm and I have not even got anywhere to stay the night yet.

The prospect of seeing Beth later on is giving me strength. I continue my journey towards Plymouth. A little familiarisation tour around the city where I will soon be working does not do any harm. For the moment I am not looking for anything permanent so I opt to spend a few nights in the Travelodge which is situated close to my new work place, on a small industrial estate. In fact my new office is literally less than a hundred meters away from the lodge. Luckily the budget hotel has got a room available, and despite the holiday season I am able to negotiate a reasonably good rate.

As the weather is beautiful I simply drop my suitcase and go out again. It is time for me to find a place for lunch. There is a pub just below the Travelodge. They are serving a wholesome Sunday roast which is ideal. I walk down to The Fox & Rabbit, watching all the happy couples and lively families enjoying themselves on the sunny patio. The pub is located alongside a busy roundabout. It is extremely noisy. While waiting for my meal I phone Justin. "I've done it," I report proudly. Justin finds it hard to hear me. "Done what? Sold your cottage?" my friend wants to know. "Well, no, that'll be next but I've moved out! I'm just outside of my Travelodge having a cold beer, and I am going to Crantock this evening to clinch the deal on the cottage," I say confidently. "Good, good," is Justin's reaction. He is at work. I can hear phones ringing in the background. "Won't hold you up now. I'll ring again tomorrow. Take care, mate," I tell him and end the short call. In the meantime a hot meal has been put in front of me but I am not very hungry. I know that it will take me a very long time to get used to my freedom.

As evening approaches I am starting to feel increasingly nervous. I am trying to settle into my room, have a shower and another shave and get ready to face Brian and Beth. It is unbearably hot in the Travelodge. I can't wait to get into my air conditioned car and hit the road again. The journey seems endless tonight but as my cottage comes into view I feel sure that I am about to make the right decision. Yet again I squeeze my car behind the silver Mercedes. Due to the heavy traffic I am a little late. Making my apologies I enter the cottage. Both Beth and Brian appear happy to see me. We are shaking hands and my heart is melting instantly. Beth is looking gorgeous as usual. I find it increasingly hard to contain my feelings for her. "Nice to see you, Rob," Brian says. He leads me up into the bathroom to show me the shiny copper pipes of the brand-new, "Economy Plus" water supply system. "Well worth the money," he points out. His long slim fingers are stroking the metal tenderly. "It's a pity that they had to dig the garden up but we'll get that sorted once we are in charge," he adds quickly. I am trying to avoid eye contact with Beth who has just arrived in the bathroom.

Eventually we return to the unusually tidy lounge. "It's very kind that you took the trouble to come all the way down here this evening. I'll make it as brief as I can," Brian starts, putting his offer on the table. "My wife is going to instruct our solicitor tomorrow. As I said I will be leaving on Wednesday morning but Beth will deal with all the affairs. You can get in touch with her any time," he continues, writing several phone numbers and addresses down for me. Beth has opened a bottle of wine but I am refusing to consume any alcohol tonight. Thankfully she is keeping well away from us as Brian and I agree on the final sale price. Brian looks pleased as punch when we come to shake hands on the deal. "It's a shame that you'll have to drive such a long way home tonight. I would have liked to invite you to a pint in the pub to celebrate," he says smiling. "Another time perhaps, thank you. You will spend a lot of future holidays here, I presume," I reply politely. "Oh, yes, we most certainly will. We have fallen in love with this place. I am just hoping that our sons will enjoy it here, too," Brian confirms.

I am desperate to get away now. Once again I have to endure a rather formal hand shake from the woman I desire. It is all too much for me. I cannot wait to reach the safety of my car. Forcing myself not to behave like a spoilt teenager I drive off slowly and leave the village. That's it, all done and dusted. What a relief!

The heat in my Travelodge room is stifling and it is not possible to open the windows very far. Although I am mentally and physically exhausted I find it hard to get any sleep. The stale air in my room and the many unresolved issues on my mind keep me awake for hours. Having to be back at Launceston for 9am means an extremely early start the next morning but at least the roads are not so busy. Needless to say I fail to have any breakfast. My stomach is rumbling as I start work. Jackie is not due in until the afternoon so I have no one who could go and get me some food. Thankfully I am able to keep going and survive until lunch time. I rarely eat out when I am working but it's a matter of "needs must" today.

Once my last customer of the morning has left I make my way over to our local pub. Enjoying the sunshine with a full plate of sandwiches, taking in the view across Launceston castle and the open countryside is a treat but it feels strange. In less than four weeks' time all this will be in the past. The realisation that so much more than just my job will change hurts immensely. A couple of people wave to me as they pass by. This is a rural town where most citizens know each other, if only by sight. I shall miss them all, every one of them and I will miss my family and friends, my relatively comfortable life style. My day dreams are suddenly disturbed by the ringtone of the mobile phone in my pocket. Not checking the screen I answer the call immediately. "Hi. I've sent Brian out to the big supermarket in Newquay so it's OK to talk. Are you at work?" Beth asks. I cannot describe how happy it makes me to hear her voice. "Not at the moment. I'm having my lunch," I reply quickly. "Good, wonderful timing. Are you on your own?" Beth enquires. "Yes, I am. How are you?" I ask her trying to swallow the rest of my ham sandwich and clear my mouth. "Not good, Rob. Since we've been together I've been thinking about the future. Everything inside me is messed up," she says. "I left home yesterday. I currently live in a terribly hot room in a Travelodge at Derriford in Plymouth, close to my new work place," I whisper, checking that no one overhears our conversation. "You've what? You've left your wife, your family? Why? What happened?" Beth asks, sounding genuinely devastated. "I'm messed up, too. That's why, I guess," I explain, pushing my plate away and getting up as others occupy the tables around me. "When Brian has gone to Brussels we must get together and talk. This is a serious matter. Brian is buying the cottage and I am also considering a separation," Beth tells me. I am in the shade now, leaning against the cool granite wall of an ancient outbuilding. "I'll ring you on Wednesday afternoon," I say quickly, feeling awkward. I am not keen on holding intimate conversations in the open air. "OK, can't wait. I love you," Beth responds, seemingly aware of the delicate situation I find myself in.

Jackie sends me home in the middle of the afternoon. According to her I don't look very well so she suggests that I finish early. It suits me fine as I can do with the time to visit home, get some of my papers and documents and, most importantly, see the children.

When I park up outside of what I still call our house I spot my parents-in-law's car. I can certainly do without having to face them right now. Hesitating for just a second I resolve not to visit after all and turn around. Angie and the children are well cared for. I am trying to convince myself that it is not necessary to see them today. Driving along I have to confess that this thing called "freedom" takes a bit of getting used to, to say the least.

My next stop is the supermarket near Plymouth. I cannot afford to go out every night for something to eat. Today I have not done well. If one of my children would feed themselves like I've done I would tell them off. I am determined not to go without breakfast again, not to have my lunch at the pub each day but to make sure that I pick up something nutritious somewhere in the evenings. Scanning the shelves in the wide aisles of the supermarket I think of Beth. Just a day and a half to go and I will be able to speak to her again on the phone and maybe I will even be able to see her on Wednesday evening when Brian is away.

Having spent yet another sleepless night I decide that I must find alternative accommodation soon. I have bought the local newspaper but I am reluctant to contact any of the agencies that offer bedsits or small flats. At work I confide in Jackie by telling her that I have finally split from Angie. A fleeting smile appears on her face. "Are you seeing someone else?" she asks matter-of-factly. Her words give me cause for concern. "What are you trying to say?" I ask her. She realises that she may have overstepped the mark and avoids the answer. Then she looks at me sternly. I respect her too much, could not possibly lie to her. Feeling terribly ashamed and embarrassed I nod. Sighing Jackie puts her warm hand on my shoulder. "Look, I don't care who you are seeing. Your secret is safe with me but you must expect people asking questions," she advises me.

For the rest of the day I can't help wondering whether Angie is suspecting my infidelity as well. Suddenly I have doubts. It appears that others, apart from Jackie, have become suspicious too but my impression is that Angie believed me when I said I spent time looking at the cottage. Having left work I make another attempt to return home to see my children and fetch a batch of important documents.

This time Barbara's car is parked outside. Reluctantly I pull up behind it and get out. Walking up the drive I can hear noises from the garden. I hesitate but then I put my key into the lock of the front door and let myself in. Like a thief I creep into the lounge. Uneasily I make my way over to our filing cabinet. As we have never bothered with curtains for the window facing the back garden I am able to watch the scene outside. Angie and Barbara are sitting in easy chairs, Melanie is crawling around the lawn and Jordan is chasing Barbara's daughters who have run off with his beloved football. As fast as I can I stuff all the papers that I want into my briefcase.

I am about to make my escape when Jordan spots me. "Dad!" he exclaims and comes running into the lounge. "Hi, son. I've missed you," I tell him. The two girls stop at the door, looking on. "Have you come back to stay with us?" Jordan wants to know. "No, I'll have to go now but I promise I'll pop in again soon," I say and it breaks my heart.

In the meantime the adults have noticed me, too. "You could have at least told us that you are here," Angie says, assessing me angrily. "I'm sorry," I reply immediately, admittedly not a great response but still… Clutching my briefcase I walk towards her. "I'd like to see Melanie before I leave, please," I demand firmly. Barbara is holding her in her arms. My little daughter has recognised me and she is smiling happily. The whole atmosphere feels so uncomfortable, all of a sudden so tense. "I want us to agree on certain times if you want to visit the children. You can't just walk in here like this," Angie suggests. I resist another "I'm sorry". Melanie is now struggling in Barbara's arms. She clearly wants to come to me. Angie's gaze is directed towards my briefcase. "My solicitor has asked for your address. You will receive quite a lot of paperwork in the next few days," Angie says bluntly. She signals to her friend to hand the hyperactive Melanie over to me. Cuddling my daughter I explain that I am staying in a Travelodge and that I have any personal mail sent to the car dealership at the moment. Angie nods but does not comment.

My house does not feel like home anymore. Within fifteen minutes I am back in my car. Somehow I am shattered. I am not cut out for this "freedom" business. Just as I am half way down the road my mobile is ringing. Sighing I pull in. It's Justin. He is still full of enthusiasm for entering golf tournaments with me. "I've got the forms ready. All you need to do is say yes," Justin urges me. "I'm by the road side, mate. I can't possibly think about it now. Let me get back to you later on," I reply, watching the traffic shoot past my car and making it shake violently in the process. "OK. Hey, you sound stressed out. How are you doing?" my friend suddenly asks. "You are right. I'm not coping well at all," I confess in a soft voice. "In that case I'll jump in the car and come up to see you. Give me an hour and a half. Where do you want us to meet?" Justin enquires immediately. I am feeling hungry so I suggest the pub below my Travelodge. "Great, my SATNAV will find it. See you later," Justin agrees.

Shaking my head I drive off. This cannot go on for too much longer. I will have to settle down. If there is no chance of returning home then I must start afresh, now, well, before I am due to start work at my new firm.

As I park my car outside the Travelodge dark clouds are moving in on the horizon, looks like our recent spell of lovely weather is about to come to an end. I go to my room to get changed. It'll be nice to see Justin and have a chat, man to man. I really appreciate him driving all the way up here, just to talk to me. Presumably he's been working all day and even at the best of times it will take him a lot more than an hour on the road each way.

Justin and I are having a brilliant evening. It has started to rain and we can hear the odd rumble of thunder in the distance. We sit by a large window overlooking the car park and we are having a good discussion. So far I have not mentioned Beth to him. "You'll be able to afford a decent flat in this area when you've sold your cottage," Justin says. I watch his long well-tanned fingers fiddle with a round beer mat on the table. My head bowed I nod but he can see that I am not looking too happy. "Do you miss Angie?" he asks me then. "Not as much as I miss the kids," I admit slowly. Justin does not have any children of his own so he can't possibly imagine what I am going through. "You should find yourself another woman, Robby. That is what you need," Justin finally suggests. "I already have," I let it slip - big mistake - but it's too late. My friend's face looks suddenly very serious. "When? How long since?" he wants to know. "It's no good though. She's married too," I explain carefully. "Wow. You never fail to surprise me. Tell me about her," Justin demands, getting quite excited by his standards.

Time is ticking on. I have had too many pints and I tell him the story of meeting Beth. "Now you will understand why my life is in such a mess," I eventually say. "Yes," Justin simply replies. "I'm hoping to see Beth tomorrow evening," I tell him, looking at my watch. "Do you know what the time is?" I ask him then. "Time for me to drive home, I expect. Judy won't be too pleased if I walk in after midnight," Justin responds. "I'm sorry. I've kept you by far too long," I apologise quickly. "It's OK. I'll give her a ring in a minute. Perhaps you could let me know about the tournament entries in the morning when you've had time to think about it all," my friend says. "Yes, of course. I'll send you a message before I start work. Take care on the road and thanks so much for coming along to listen. I appreciate it," I reply. The time has come to see him off. Dodging vast puddles in the car park I make my way back to the Travelodge.

The long awaited Wednesday is another miserable day. We have had rain and fog for most of the morning. It is one of those wet days when hardly anyone visits the showroom. I am having lunch with Jackie in the White Horse Inn, my invitation. We are about to tuck in when my phone rings. Thinking it could well be Beth I jump up and leave the table, in fact, there is a rule in this pub stating that mobile phone calls are to be held outside.

So here I am getting soaked to the skin, watching grey wads of mist pass by. "He's gone. What time are you coming?" Beth asks me excitedly. "In this weather I won't be arriving until about 8pm, if that's OK," I reply, looking around the deserted car park in front of the pub. Beth tells me that there is not much rain in Crantock and certainly no fog. "Great, I can't wait. Will you have to go to work in the morning or will you be able to take half a day off?" Beth enquires. "I'll see what I can do," I promise, hoping that Jackie will be able to cope on her own for one morning, considering I have just bought her lunch.

With that I return to the table. "Sorry," I apologise. Jackie has cleared her plate. She does not say anything but I can tell from the look in her eyes that she can guess who the caller was. Knowing that I cannot put it off I ask my colleague to look after the showroom without me tomorrow morning and she is surprisingly accommodating. "Fine, as long as you work on Sunday instead," she agrees.

Somehow my newly found freedom makes me feel nervous. Perhaps it is the excitement, the thought of eating a forbidden fruit, I don't know. Whatever it is, I can't wait to leave work in good time. Butterflies in my stomach I drive straight to the Travelodge. Wasting no time I get changed and pack a few belongings into a holdall. Although I am physically prepared for my trip to Crantock I cannot quite conquer the nasty demons inside my head. I know I should not be making this journey. I should be telling Beth that I have had second thoughts, that I cannot continue with this little romance, that I don't want an affair – but, of course, I do no such thing. I am already sitting in my car, key in the ignition, ready to go. At least the weather has improved considerably. Turning up my car radio to high volume I drive along the A38. Dismissing any further doubts I am beginning to enjoy myself. I am dreaming of the hours ahead as I pass Bodmin where Justin lives, and I just can't wait to see Beth.

Now that Brian's large Mercedes has gone my VW fits neatly into the space on the road side in front of my cottage. I have been trying to keep to the speed limit but there were no hold-ups and I've arrived in record time. "Rob, darling! It's you! I was wondering who was coming to see me this time of day," she greets me as she opens the door. I take her into my arms. Holding and kissing her is the most wonderful feeling. Beth pulls me into the lounge. "Have you had dinner yet?" she wants to know. "No," I reply, my eyes scanning the papers that are spread out all over the floor. "What's this?" I enquire, pointing at a set of drawings. "Oh, that's what Brian has done all day yesterday," Beth replies vaguely, quickly picking up the sheets. "Let's have a look," I demand but Beth refuses. "The deal is done, darling. You will have to let Brian do what he wants to," she says, hiding the papers in the old wooden cupboard. "Is that what you want as well?" I ask. "It doesn't matter anymore what I want. I have decided to leave Brian once the holidays are over," she tells me. "But you said you wouldn't even consider breaking his heart," I remind her. "Well, I've changed my mind. Since you left that Sunday afternoon my world has been turned upside down. As I explained to you before, I don't want an affair. It's not good for me or my work," Beth says, making her way to the tiny kitchen. I am staggered, totally shocked, so I follow her around like a dog. "You are rushing things, Beth," I remark, a little unsure how to handle the situation. "My books are successful, Rob. I can easily afford to live by myself. There was a time when I was heavily dependent on Brian's wealth but no longer. I have realised that I can break free whenever I want to," she says while preparing a meal for us. "OK, so what are your plans?" I want to know, feeling most uncomfortable with her drastic decision. "I can't continue cheating on Brian. It's not what I want, not my style. I can't bear his touch anymore, can't love him anymore," Beth tries to explain.

Taking in a deep breath I pull up one of the wonky kitchen chairs and sit down. I have to admit, I had not expected this. "I have no right to destroy your marriage," I say quickly. Beth laughs out loud. "It's not a question of rights, Rob. We've done what we've done because it was meant to happen. I honestly believe that," she insists, rapidly stirring the contents of a large saucepan in front of her. "You've left your family because of what has happened. Don't tell me otherwise," Beth points out sternly. Then she instructs me to open a bottle of wine and get our plates ready. "You are going to sell this cottage to Brian because you want to see me. You've negotiated tomorrow morning off because you want to spend the night with me. I know exactly how you tick," she says pompously. Again, I draw in breath and I shake my head. "Your children are a lot older than mine but you should consider them, too. It's too early to leave everything behind. Two nights and two days are not enough to change our lives!" I shout at her. "Is that how you feel about it? You want sex but no commitment, an affair but nothing more? If that is what you think then I would suggest you go home right now," she responds furiously.

Of course, Beth is correct. That is what I should be doing but I say: "You are moving too fast for me, Beth, that's all." I am trying to stand my ground. The Hendersons' tendency to bully me is working me up the wrong way. I've been looking forward to coming here, to relax and forget my problems for a while but all of a sudden this relationship is becoming more stressful than my marriage. Beth passes me my food but my appetite has disappeared. Downing my first glass of wine as fast as I can I follow her back into the lounge. "Give us time, please," I plead. In the soft golden light of the candle that Beth has lit for us I can see tears streaming down her pretty face. I take her hand and stroke it tenderly. "I'm sorry. I did not mean to upset you," I apologise sincerely. "Eat!" she commands angrily, quite obviously struggling to enjoy the meal herself.

In silence we have our dinner. "I am going to leave Crantock tomorrow. Don't worry, I'll pay for the accommodation until 31st August as agreed but I think I'll need to return home, sooner rather than later," Beth announces suddenly. "Why? I was hoping to see you while

96

Brian is away," I answer immediately. Unexpectedly I am finding this evening increasingly difficult. "Come on, let's go for a walk, get some fresh air. I don't like to see you in this mood," I propose quickly.

We empty our glasses, extinguish the by now badly dripping candle and leave the cottage. As always we don't touch while strolling along the road towards the beach. The village is still busy with tourists. To avoid the steady traffic we decide to turn into a side road which leads to the highest part of the coast path. The evening sun is setting beautifully on the horizon. We take our sandals off in readiness to climb down the high dunes. Tonight the soft sand feels refreshingly cool under foot. Within seconds we have reached the beach. From down here the vast expanse of golden sand looks so impressive. We stop for a moment to listen to the waves, their strong and powerful evensong - rhythmic, mysterious and strangely calming. "I hate secrecy, Rob. I'd like to show my feelings for you in public. I'd like to come clean with Brian, with the boys. I can't live a life of lies. I don't like the tension," Beth explains as we walk through the firm sand towards the water's edge. Soon we proceed further into the ocean, up to our ankles. I know that Beth is right, I understand what she means but I don't feel like agreeing with her. Overcome by emotions I stop walking instantly, take her firmly into my arms and kiss her like I've never kissed anyone before. Despite it all my desire for her is burning strongly inside me. It has done the trick. Beth's face looks so much happier again. Gasping for breath after another long kiss she wriggles herself free. "Time to return to the cottage, I think," she whispers seductively. Arm in arm we walk on for a while. It is so pleasant on the beach tonight that we decide to go back the usual way, past the surf school and the ice-cream hut. Both establishments have closed hours ago but we are trying to extend the sunset experience for a little longer.

The magic of this beach makes me lose my inhibitions. On our way back I insist on holding Beth's hand. "Do you seriously believe there's anyone around who knows us?" I ask confidently, kicking up some heavy damp sand with my bare feet. "Yes, the neighbour who fixed the pipes the other day, the lady from the vicarage who chats to me every morning, the man in the post office and shop – they all recognise me by now," Beth says smiling. It does not take long until we reach the foot of the high dunes, the place where hundreds of day visitors have created to clear path to the top. Before we leave this wonderful beach behind for the night I want to kiss Beth once more. Again I take her into my arms and kiss her passionately. I can't wait to make love to her. Slowly I let her go, our hands still joined.

As we look up to the top of the steep dune we spot a lonely figure standing right at the summit, watching us. There is nowhere to go as disaster strikes. Brian Henderson, dressed in a light blue cotton shirt, dark trousers and fine leather brogues, does not fit into this romantic picture of beach babes and holiday-makers. He does not move an inch as we approach. I have never felt so humiliated in my entire life.

"Brian, what are you doing here?" Beth asks nervously. "I could ask you the same question but I have seen quite clearly what you were doing," Brian answers, a thunderous expression on his aging face. The slight evening breeze makes me shiver – or is it that horrible feeling of utter shame and embarrassment? "My meeting was cancelled so I thought I'd return to my holidays," Brian explains calmly. I am rooted to the spot, standing next to Beth but no longer holding her hand. "I'm sorry, Brian, I should have told you," Beth says then. "Yes, if you'd had any decency you would have done," Brian responds. His cool expression does not change. "I have often suspected that my wife would one day be unfaithful to me but I am disgusted to think that she has chosen someone like you," Brian says to me. I have difficulty showing restraint but I am determined not to lose my dignity completely tonight. "A man with a lovely wife and a young family!" Brian continues. "Please, Brian, let us discuss this elsewhere, not out here," Beth begs. She appears strangely calm whereas I wish I could simply vanish from the face of this earth.

"Looks like Rob will have to collect his bag from the cottage anyway," Brian remarks while climbing down the dune towards the lower beach car park. Beth and I follow in silence. The road back to my property seems so long this evening. I cannot describe how I feel, definitely one notch better than being found in bed with Beth but this is certainly bad enough. No words are spoken as the three of us march along the tarmac.

Beth has decided to lead the way. She pulls her key out of her shorts and lets us enter the cottage. As fast as I can I grab my holdall and my car keys. All I want is flee from this dreadful scene. I sense that Brian is absolutely fuming but he says nothing. He simply proceeds into the lounge, allowing his wife to see me off. Lost for words I carry my bag to the car with Beth walking behind me. "I'm so sorry, Rob. I had no idea that this would happen. I will be in touch as soon as I can," she promises. "Don't. Forget it, please. It is no good," is all I can say and then I am off, hurrying to the safety of my car. I drive off, shaking like a leaf.

It is unbelievable how many different thoughts have gone through my mind since last night. I can barely remember how I got back to the Travelodge but I obviously did. My life has reached a point where things can hardly get worse. Having the morning off, after such a restless night, is bliss though. I am able to have my breakfast in the pub without the need to rush. Although I have some spare time today I am not making any effort to sort my future out. I am feeling terribly low. My thoughts are with Beth who no doubt has had a difficult night with Brian, too. To be perfectly honest, my biggest fear is that she is going to leave him and then expects to live with me. I am not sure if I want that, not yet, not at all, I don't know - it's all too quick, too soon. I wish we had never had that weekend together, those wonderful, incredible two nights and two days, this unforgettable romance. It was a one-off, a lovely dream but for it to continue our lives would have to change so completely, and at present I certainly don't feel ready for it. All I want is normality and stability to return to my life. I want to get back to where I was three months ago, at home with my wife and my children, at work with Jackie and all my friends and colleagues in Launceston, competing in golf tournaments with Justin - but now I've lost it all. I have nothing left. Apart from starting a new job soon my life is empty, complicated and depressing. I am crying for help but there is none. I am on my own in this twisted world that I have created for myself.

Today I am having my lunch at my desk at work. As I bite into my sandwich Jackie catches up with me. "I am organising your leaving party," she says, taking a seat opposite me, pen and note pad poised. "I don't want one," I reply sharply. "You've got to have it and I'd like to know if there is anyone else you want me to invite - friends, former colleagues, whoever - and what about your wife and your family?" Jackie asks, already scribbling something onto the pad. Thinking about it for a moment I am wondering if I should get her to invite Justin and Judy but then I dismiss the idea, considering that they would have to come quite a long way just for a small party. Nervously playing with the sandwich packaging I respond: "Yes, I'd like you to invite Angie. She may have to bring Jordan and Melanie but there's no one else I can think of." I am trying hard to continue eating but Jackie is meticulous in her preparations. All through my lunch hour I have to answer questions. I am more than relieved when I eventually start work and have the chance to be out of the office on a couple of test drives this afternoon.

There has been quite a lot of mail for me today as well. I have received solicitors' letters both regarding the sale of the cottage and my divorce, besides there are invoices from the plumber and a letter from the letting agent in Newquay. Reluctantly I scan the correspondence and then let it disappear into my briefcase. I resolve to pop in what Angie's solicitor calls our "matrimonial home" to visit my children on the way back to Plymouth. As I am in charge of locking up the showroom tonight I am unable to leave as early as I originally intended but once I get into my car my mobile phone rings. "Rob, it's Brian Henderson," a confident voice greets me. Rolling my eyes heavenwards I reply: "Hi." "I am withdrawing my offer and have instructed my solicitor to abort the purchase," Beth's husband tells me. "I understand," I stutter, unsure what to say next but Brian has already ended the call. Tomorrow I will talk to the letting agent, and once I have terminated the contract with him I will put the cottage on the market. The sooner I can get rid of the place, the better.

I drive off, hoping that Angie and the children will be at home. Nervously but quite positively, I approach our house. As soon as I ring the door bell any joyful anticipation turns into fear. After a few seconds I pull out my key and try to let myself in. To my great surprise I get absolutely nowhere. Angie must have changed the lock! To say that I am furious is an understatement. Repeatedly I ring the bell but there is no answer. Eventually I have to give up and leave. It seems that Angie won't let me have access to the kids anymore unless by prior arrangement. Disappointed and sad I get back into my car. For minutes I just sit there waiting, hoping that my family may return but it is all in vain.

The last thing I want is go back to the lonely Travelodge right now but, of course, I have nowhere else to go and I need to get changed before I can go out for dinner. Much slower than usual I drive back to Plymouth. I realise that I have to start getting a grip on the situation before I end up in a mental hospital.

Turning into the car park of the Travelodge I do not notice the elegant black sports car which has been parked up right at the other end of the large marked-out area. All I see is a figure running towards my car as I lock it. "Rob, darling!" a by now very familiar voice shouts. I turn around and there is Beth. "What are you doing here?" I ask, genuinely surprised to see her. "I am free, Rob, free. I've left Brian and it feels fine," she says happily, smiling in her own special way. Instantly I wish I'd never told her that I am currently residing at the Derriford Travelodge. "Aren't you pleased to see me?" Beth wants to know. I am not actually but I can't bring myself to say so. My briefcase in one hand, the car keys in the other, I wonder how to handle her. "I'll invite you to dinner," Beth offers then. "Thanks," is all I say.

Silently Beth and I walk towards the reception area. What I really want is tell her to leave me alone but all I do is get my key card out as usual and let us into the secure part of the building. Then we pass along the seemingly endless corridor together until we reach my room. Once the door is closed behind us Beth takes me into her arms. "This is a dream come true. I am with you," she whispers. I am hesitating, can't even kiss her. Here I am, in a hotel room with the woman I have experienced the most amazing sex with and my body feels rigid like a board. Her warm fingers are stroking my neck. "I love you, Rob. I am ready to be with you day and night," she tells me tenderly. It's too much for me. I am feeling bullied again and I don't like it. Decisively I push her away. "Listen, Beth. It's not that simple," I tell her firmly. "It is, darling, very simple. Come here, sit down, relax," she says, taking my hand and pulling me over to my double bed. Like lightning her small hands get hold of the buckle of my belt. Her hot lips are caressing mine. I collapse into the fresh white bedding, taking the weight of my beautiful mistress with me in the process. Torn between doubt and desire I lie there, unable to do what she expects of me. Undeterred by my passivity she begins to undress me. I can no longer resist, it feels so good. I have never met anyone quite like her.

My mind is telling me to stop, to send her away but my body is craving love. A few minutes later my doubts are rapidly disappearing. I shut out my fears and go for it. Our sexual reunion is fast, lacking proper emotion. "I'm sorry," I apologise immediately. "Sorry for what?" Beth enquires, smiling at me. My hands are lovingly gliding over her gorgeous body. "For rushing, not taking my time," I reply truthfully. "It's fine. I was just as desperate as you were," she replies softly. "Let's go out. We need to talk," I suggest then. I am swapping my suit trousers for a pair of jeans and put a clean shirt on with Beth watching. Once she has got her clothes back on, she takes over. "I've seen this delightful little restaurant earlier when I was driving around. If it is open tonight I'd like to take you there," she says and she adds: "I've also had a look at your new firm earlier. Great place, nice cars. I am sure you will like it there!" I make no comment but follow her to her Mercedes. Smiling triumphantly she drives off. "I hope I will find that restaurant again," she says nervously, not looking quite so confident now.

Less than half an hour later we are entering a very cosy, quite exclusive restaurant. I have no idea how Beth has come across it. It is hidden away in a courtyard, off the main road. Beth has parked her car in a public car park and we have had to walk through several streets to get here. It is an expensive eatery, not the kind of place I would have chosen. Our casual attire does not go down too well either. However, there are so few other customers around that the waiter is prepared to accept us as we are. Beth looks happy. She is smiling but I am rather serious at the moment.

Pretending to study the menu intensely I buy myself some time. I don't know what to say, how to react to this rather uncomfortable scenario of having to deal with Beth tonight. Suddenly I feel her warm fingers touching mine tenderly. "Why are you still wearing your wedding ring?" she asks me. "Because I'm still married," I reply, slowly dropping the menu down onto the pristine white table cloth. Beth withdraws her hand. "So am I but I left my ring with Brian. I don't want to be married to him any longer," she says firmly. She sounds like a stubborn child. Her determination to make a new start worries me. I can see the waiter hovering so I decide not to talk about private matters anymore. We order our food and a bottle of wine. "I'll only have one glass, I am driving," Beth explains. She is obviously set on making me drunk. "And I've got to go to work in the morning," I respond, yawning. "Have you had a tough day?" Beth asks, assessing the strained expression on my face. I nod silently. Every day is a tough day since I've left home, to be honest but yet again I don't say it aloud. "I'll go back to Surrey for a few days tomorrow, just to sort various matters out before the boys are returning from America," she tells me. I still cannot quite believe that she has left Brian so suddenly but perhaps he has kicked her out.

After a couple of glasses of excellent wine I am beginning to relax. The food is fantastic, too – best meal I've had in ages. There is so much I meant to talk to Beth about but being in charge of drinking most of the bottle changes my resolve. I am enjoying Beth's company, the undivided attention she pays me, her free spirit and her laughter. I know it is wrong but after a while I am able to forget my problems and my family, if only for a short time. Naturally, I offer to pay the bill. Beth shakes her head. "I said that it would be my treat tonight and I mean it," she insists. Shrugging my shoulders I thank her, feeling very light-headed.

Once Beth has settled up we leave the restaurant. This is the moment when I am supposed to be telling her that I want her to rent her own room in the Travelodge but I do absolutely nothing. I simply jump in the passenger seat of her Mercedes and let her drive off. "Lovely place, we must come here again some time," she remarks happily. We have a hard job to find our way back to the lodge in the dark. "How long are you intending to stay here?" Beth asks when we finally arrive in the car park. "I don't know," is my honest reply. Just as Beth leans over from the driver's seat to kiss me my mobile rings. I am surprised to see on the phone's display that the caller is Angie. Reluctantly I answer the call. "Rob, I am sorry to trouble you this time of night but Jordan has had an accident," Angie starts. If I felt intoxicated two minutes ago, then I am sober as a judge now. "What happened?" I want to know. "He was playing football with friends and had a bad fall. To begin with we didn't think it was too serious but I had to take him to hospital around 6pm. We've spent hours in the Minor Injuries Unit but now they've sent us to Derriford. It's a complicated fracture and requires surgery," Angie informs me. I can feel the blood draining out of my face. "Jordan has asked me to ring you. He wants you to come," Angie tells me. "Yes, of course," I respond, fully aware that I am no more than a ten minute walk away from the large hospital. Driving would be out of the question tonight anyway. "Where's Melanie?" I enquire then. "She's with Barbara at the moment. I didn't want to worry my parents at this stage," Angie explains. I nod silently. Beth, sitting upright in the driver's seat, is signalling to me that she is prepared to drive wherever I need to go. "I'll meet you at the hospital as soon as I can," I eventually confirm, unsure if I should be grateful for Beth's offer or not. "Thanks," Angie simply says before explaining where to find Jordan's ward in the vast hospital building.

I finish the call, totally drained with concern for my young son. Beth has taken my hand, having overheard the conversation. "OK, darling, let's go," she says, squeezing my fingers encouragingly and starting the engine again. "I'm sorry, I am spoiling the evening. I can easily walk..." I mutter nervously. "Don't be silly, Rob. You seem to forget that I've got children, too. I know exactly how you are feeling. I'll get you there right now," Beth says. Within five minutes we have reached the hospital car park. It is such a relief to have a confident driver in this situation, someone who understands my emotions. During the short journey Beth has kept me talking, trying to keep me calm.

"I'll wait in the car," she offers. "Please go back to the lodge. I don't know how long I will be," I reply. With that I pull the key card for my room out of my pocket and hand it to Beth. "Don't worry. I'll stay here until you return. I can always come in. They must have a coffee shop or something in a large hospital like this. Now, go – good luck!" she encourages me. I leave the car and jog over to the main entrance.

It is a long way to Jordan's ward and I am so nervous that I almost get lost but eventually I find the right place. A young nurse leads me to my son's bed. "Dad!" Jordan exclaims happily. In the bright neon light he looks pale and so does his mother. "Thanks for coming so quickly, Rob," she greets me. She is sitting in a visitor's chair next to Jordan's bed, not moving from our boy's side. "They are waiting for a theatre to become available," Angie explains, holding Jordan's cold hand. "Are you in a lot of pain?" I ask my son. "Not too bad," he responds bravely but I can tell that he is very scared. "I have been told that I will be able to stay at the hospital for a couple of days until Jordan is ready to come home with me. I was wondering if you could get me a few things from home and look after Melanie," Angie says. She is passing me a list that she has written earlier. "Yes, of course," I agree immediately but Angie frowns. "Have you been drinking?" she asks. "Yes, I've been out with a friend," I reply casually, feeling somewhat embarrassed. "A friend? Judging by your breath you shouldn't have been driving," Angie points out. I am hoping that she will not be asking any questions about my friend. Trying hard not to tell lies I explain: "My friend drove me." Angie's ashen face appears even paler than before. "Where is he now? Is he waiting for you?" she enquires carefully.

Looking at my son I don't have the guts to tell Angie that my driver is female.

Before I can come up with any further explanations a nurse arrives to prepare Jordan for his operation. "Right, soldier, I think we'll get your leg fixed before the day is out," she says cheerfully. Both Angie and I have temporarily forgotten how late it is. Angie looks absolutely shattered, totally exhausted. "You must have a rest now," the blond nurse advises her caringly. "Well, I could do with a strong coffee to start with," Angie replies softly. I offer immediately to organise one for her but she insists on doing it herself. "You'd better get back to that friend of yours. I am sure he does not want to wait all night to take you back," Angie says to me as two porters arrive to take Jordan to theatre. My poor little son looks so frightened. I kiss his head and squeeze his hand just like Beth has done to me earlier to give me encouragement but it does not help. Jordan is being wheeled off and Angie walks along the corridor with the porters for a while, not wanting to let him go, before eventually returning to me.

"My stuff will have to wait until tomorrow. I don't expect your friend will be able to get you to Barbara's at this time of night. I was hoping Barb and Charles would not have to look after Melanie for this long. I think I will give Barb a ring and tell her that you will be coming to pick her up first thing in the morning. You can take her home, give her a bath and feed her. Here are the keys," Angie says. She passes me an unfamiliar looking pouch containing shiny new keys. Taking it from her I invite her to have a coffee with me before she makes the call. Then I put my arms around her to comfort her. "Jordan will be fine," I tell her confidently. For once Angie is not fighting me off, in fact she holds me tight. We are standing in the long brightly lit corridor and I can feel my wife's tears creating wet patches on my cotton shirt. It's breaking my heart. Why can't we be together like this always? My hands are stroking her back but inevitably my mind is on Beth who is outside in her luxury car patiently waiting for me.

I am tempted to kiss Angie but last minute I decide against it. "Listen, you go and ring Barbara and I'll order us two coffees," I suggest, hoping not to bump into Beth in the cafeteria. Angie nods gratefully before following me out of the ward. While she is leaving the building to use her mobile, I hurry to locate the coffee shop. It is already five minutes past midnight and I have absolutely no idea how long I've been in the hospital. To my surprise the cafeteria has closed for the night but there are several slot machines offering drinks. Thankfully, I find some loose coins in my jeans pockets and I am able to purchase a couple of hot coffees.

Looking around nervously I cannot see Beth anywhere. The last thing I want is for her to accidentally bump into Angie outside. A sudden urge to get some fresh air sends me out into the cool dark forecourt where my wife is. "I've spoken to Barbara. Melanie is sleeping. Barbara thinks she will be fine with them until you pick her up early tomorrow morning. You must get your friend to drive you back now, Rob. The poor chap won't want to be up all night. Doesn't he have a family?" Angie enquires. I ignore her question deliberately and insist on sitting down together first. My wife is shivering. "Have you had any dinner tonight?" I ask her, pulling her back into the uncomfortably warm hospital building. "No," she replies slowly. "Sit down, I'll get you a sandwich from the machine," I offer, walking off. Angie drops into one of the poorly upholstered chairs in the lobby, clutching her cardboard mug.

As I hand the sandwich over to her I wish I could stay with her. I have never seen her look so empty and sad. "I'll take you back to the ward before I go," I say helplessly, watching her eat. "How long do you reckon it'll take to pin Jordan's leg?" I ask her for something to say. Angie is shaking her head. "I don't know. It doesn't really matter. I'll be up until he gets back anyway," she replies and she adds: "Thanks for being here tonight, Rob but you can go now. There is nothing more you can do for the moment. I would just be grateful if you could deliver my things later on and look after Melanie. That's all."

I hate to leave her but eventually I decide that it would be wise for me to escape before Angie can ask any further questions. "I would prefer to stay, obviously…," I say softly, putting my arm around her again. Angie nods. I feel that she would like me to stay too which makes it even harder. Slowly we walk up the stairs to the third floor. It is quiet on the ward now. A couple of nurses are busy with paperwork behind a large desk, acknowledging us briefly. "I'll be back as soon as I can," I promise. "Please send me a message when Jordan is back on the ward," I continue. With that I take my wife into my arms once more and kiss her quickly.

Back in Beth's car I collapse into the passenger seat. "You must be tired," I remark, yawning. "I'm fine, darling. If there's anything I can do for you, I will," she confirms smiling. "Thanks, but I think we must both try and get a couple of hours sleep, at least," I respond. Something in the back of my mind tells me that I am supposed to encourage Beth to get her own room for the night but as I have already given her my key card I decide that this is not the time or the place for a discussion about our future. Beth starts the engine. I am by far too nervous to even close my eyes for a second and I feel pretty worn out. We hardly speak on the way back to the lodge.

As we arrive at the Travelodge Beth naturally follows me to my room, not expecting anything else but to share my bed for the next few hours, of course. Silently we get undressed. Minutes later, not leaving my mobile phone out of sight, I climb under the sheets, waiting for Angie to contact me with news of Jordan.

Beth joins me, stroking and kissing me tenderly but not demanding any attention. "Everything will be fine," she whispers lovingly. She has been so good to me tonight but I just cannot give her much in return. While I am lying awake, thinking of Jordan, Beth falls asleep next to me. At 3am I finally receive the long-awaited text from Angie. "Jordan OK, very sleepy. See you later," it reads. Feeling relieved I cuddle into Beth and fall asleep instantly.

My first task when I wake up is to ring Jackie and explain that I'll need a couple of days off, unpaid if necessary. Beth insists on having breakfast with her but there is no time. I have promised to be at Barbara and Charles' house by 9am to take Melanie off their hands. "You go and have your breakfast, Beth. I'll have mine at the hospital," I tell her. "OK, I understand. I'll be off home later on but I'll be back, next weekend at the latest," she says, kissing me. I make no comment. My head is hurting and I am in a rush. Frankly, I'll be glad to get rid of her for a while. This affair is just too much for me at the moment.

It is not easy when I arrive at Barbara and Charles's house either. I am not in their best books, to put it mildly. Having been given a rather cool reception by my wife's best friend I can't wait to see my little daughter. She still recognises me, I am sure. "Dada, Dad," she says smiling as I kiss her wildly. Thankfully Charles is off to work soon. He won't speak to me anymore. "We'll be coming to visit Jordan later on this afternoon," Barbara says, handing Melanie and her few belongings over to me. "She's been an absolute delight – no problem at all," Barbara confirms, playing with my daughter's small fingers. "Thanks for looking after her," I respond awkwardly. Barbara smiles politely but I sense that she does not like me much better than her husband does.

I am relieved when Melanie is finally in my car. She is chuckling away to herself on the way home. Before returning to Plymouth I will have to collect everything that Angie has put on her list. Entering our property feels very strange. Inside the house nothing has changed but the pain inside my chest is quite incredible. For a minute I simply stand in the middle of the lounge and look around. There is nothing I want more than come back here to live with my family.

Trying to occupy Melanie and packing a bag for Angie at the same time I wonder what I can do to mend the large cracks in my marriage. What has happened has happened. I cannot undo the mistakes I have made. I am tempted to search the filing cabinet for Angie's divorce papers, just to read what she tells her solicitor about me but there is simply not enough time to snoop around.

As instructed by Angie I bathe and feed my daughter and then we hit the road again. At this time of the morning we are faced with heavy traffic. My stomach is rumbling badly, in fact I am not feeling so good at all. I am overtired and I have a bit of a hangover which is hardly surprising.

It is another beautiful day today, hot already and it is still mid-morning. I am driving along with a thousand questions on my mind. Melanie has gone quiet but the smell coming from the back of the car indicates that she will require a nappy change at the earliest possible opportunity. I have to let the windows down as the dense traffic has just come to a stand-still. The 25-mile trip to Derriford seems like a long-haul to me this morning.

Eventually we arrive at the hospital. Melanie is feeling uncomfortable and I am starving. I decide to get my daughter changed in the car park first before going anywhere. As always, passers-by give me strange looks.

What is wrong with a caring father cleaning up his child? I bet if Angie was doing what I am doing right now no one would worry in the slightest but Melanie certainly knows how to embarrass me in public. She is wriggling and kicking on her changing mat and I am trying patiently to stamp my authority on her without making her cry.

Laden with Angie's bag in one arm, my little daughter in the other, I arrive at Jordan's ward. Melanie is even more pleased to see her mother than I am. I can hardly contain her. Angie, still in the clothes she wore yesterday, is looking stressed and tired. "Great to see you, Dad," Jordan greets me. He is very pale but at least he is smiling. "How are you feeling this morning?" I want to know, kissing him. "Not too good," Angie answers on his behalf. "The anaesthetic made him sick and his leg is very sore," she explains. "Poor kid," is all I can say. "Thanks for bringing my clothes. I'd like to go and have a shower and freshen up a bit while you are with Jordan," Angie tells me. All I want is to have breakfast but I cannot deny her the chance of some personal space. Nodding agreeably I take Melanie off her again and sit down next to my son's bed.

"Is there anything you want, Jordan?" I ask him, thinking of food, toys, books or magazines. "Yes, Dad, I want you to come back home," he responds immediately. Melanie has had enough of sitting on my lap. She is struggling and wants to get down. "It's not that simple, son. If Mummy doesn't want me to then there's nothing I can do," I confess openly. "But she does, Dad. I've heard her telling Auntie Barb on the phone that she misses you," Jordan argues. My brave son is in quite a lot of pain. It shows in the way he is turning in his bed but he adds: "I miss you, too. It's so different

116

without you and I don't like it." To hear an eight year old child talk like this is heart-wrenching. I just wish there was something I could say, something I could do.

Melanie has eventually managed to break free and she is now toddling along the ward, making a nuisance of herself. I have no option but to run after her which gives me an opportunity to escape from Jordan's request for a while.

The nurses think that my little daughter is adorable but I find her really hard work at the moment. I am glad when Angie returns. She is looking much better and she takes over immediately. "I'll have to go and get myself something to eat. I've missed out on breakfast. It's such a lovely day. Why don't you and Melanie come with me? We'll find somewhere nice and have an early lunch," I suggest to my wife. We are all congregating at Jordan's bedside now. I can feel that Angie is reluctant but our son gives her the go-ahead. "You can go with Dad, Mum. I'll be OK for a couple of hours," he confirms, yawning. I am very surprised how mature Jordan is for his age.

Carrying Melanie in her arms Angie goes off to speak to the nurses and then she is prepared to accompany me.

We leave the large hospital building the hot summer sun is burning fiercely. "Good day for the beach," Angie remarks suddenly. I am instantly reminded of my property in Crantock and with that the memories of the unforgettable hours with Beth return. I nod slowly. "I'd like to buy something for Jordan – he's been incredibly brave, don't you think?" I say. "Yes, he has. Have you asked him what he would like?" Angie enquires as we get into my car. "Yes, I have but unfortunately what he wants we cannot buy," I reply carefully. "And what is that?" Angie asks. "A happy home," I answer truthfully.

There is an awkward moment of silence. I don't think Angie knows what to say to that. Before I start the engine I put my mobile into the small console by the gear stick. I should have switched the thing off because just as I turn out of the busy car park it rings. In the past I would have asked Angie to answer it but a quick glace at the numbers displayed on the tiny screen tells me that the caller is Beth. "Leave it," I say sharply, afraid that my wife may pick it up like she used to. Sternly I drive on, hoping that the annoying ring tone will cease. When it finally does Angie suddenly says: "That's an idea – why don't we buy Jordan a mobile phone? I know we decided before that he is still a little too young to handle a phone but he will be nine later this year and if we get him a cheap mobile with pay-as-you-go credit he will soon learn not to spend too much money on texts and calls. Whenever he needs to he can ring either you or me. What do you think?" I think that owning a mobile phone does not make up for a broken home but, of course, I don't say that. All I do is tell Angie that it is a brilliant idea and with that I am trying desperately to find a parking space near one of the many mobile phone shops in Plymouth's city centre.

Not having had any breakfast does not help my mood. I want the phone purchase over and done with as quickly as possible so that we can have lunch somewhere. Angie, however, takes her time choosing the right phone for Jordan. I feel like a spare part standing in the middle of an ultra modern phone shop, a crying Melanie in my arms, while my wife is negotiating the best price on an already heavily discounted device. She is arguing with the less than helpful sales assistant and I am nearly collapsing due to lack of food.

Outside the shop it is boiling hot, noisy and dusty. I wish I could be in the refreshingly cold sea, happily swimming along with Beth…Why do I think of her all of the time? I am trying to get her out of my mind but I can't, just can't. Melanie is getting more and more irritable, forcing me to take her back to the car while Angie pays for the phone.

Having put my daughter back into her car seat I am wondering if I have time to phone Beth back but then I spot my wife finally leaving the shop. Angie seems pleased with her purchase. Thankfully, we can look for a restaurant now. It does not take us long to find a pub with a shady beer garden. Although the outside area is extremely busy Melanie gets fixed up with a comfortable highchair which solves half of our problems. I have deliberately left my phone in the car, hoping that I will have an undisturbed conversation with my wife.

While I have quickly chosen my meal Angie is still studying the badly stained menu.

"My solicitor is waiting to hear from yours," she suddenly says. I must admit I have not prepared myself for a discussion about our divorce today. "I haven't got one yet," I confess slowly. "That's what I mean. You are delaying the process, Rob. I'd like to move on," Angie says, finally ready to order and signalling to the waitress. "What's the rush? Have you met someone?" I enquire, my mouth dry and my stomach aching. "No, but I'd like to get our affairs settled, our finances, access to the children and all that goes with it," Angie explains calmly. "Jordan seems to think that you may have changed your mind...," I start but then I can't finish as the drinks are being served. "It's tough for him, I know," Angie responds, playing with Melanie who is very well behaved at the moment. Taking a deep breath I say: "It's tough for everyone. Why don't we try – one last time – to make our relationship work?" Well, that has not been easy but now that I've said it I feel quite proud of myself.

Angie is shaking her head. "I don't know if there is any point," she says then. Looking at her now it appears to me that she is at least considering it. "Let's try it, please," I encourage her, taking her hand. The fact that she does not reject my touch gives me hope. I smile at her happily and for once she smiles back. Our reconciliation is ever so fragile but it is a start.

We are both hungry and tucking into our food. Melanie is not doing quite so well but neither of us are too worried how much she eats as long as she docs not play up. I feel like ordering champagne but that will have to wait. If I can persuade Angie to forget about a divorce I will be extremely lucky.

It is soon time for us to return to the hospital. To say that I am in a buoyant mood is an understatement. This is the best lunch hour I've had for a very long time. Angie seems less convinced that we will succeed in trying again but I will conveniently ignore that for the moment.

Back in the car my mobile shows several missed calls and messages. "I must be popular," I remark casually, turning the phone off rather than looking who the callers were. "You should at least check if there were any important messages," Angie advises strictly. "Not now. Let's get back to Jordan," I refuse and start the engine. Within ten minutes Melanie has fallen asleep in her car seat. Angie, next to me, looks a little tense and she is not talking much but I feel on top of the world.

When we get back to the ward Jordan is asleep. Having woken Melanie up Angie and I decide to go for a walk in the hospital garden. It is still incredibly hot outside. "If it's OK with you I shall check out of the Travelodge tonight and move back home," I tell Angie while Melanie is crawling along the well-kept lawn in between the flower beds. "Yes, it will be best for Melanie if she can sleep in her own bed this evening and hopefully Jordan will be able to leave hospital in the next couple of days as well. I could do with your help for a while," my wife replies. She is sitting down next to me on a wooden bench. Instinctively I put my arm around her. "We'll make our marriage work, I promise," I whisper. For a few minutes we simply cuddle up, close our eyes and enjoy the warm sunshine, however, our lively toddler ensures that we are not resting for too long. Melanie's attempts to walk for any length of time have failed and frustration is setting in. We have no choice but to rescue her from the gravel path and decide to return to the ward.

Jordan is now awake and feeling better. Angie can't wait to present him with our gift. "Thank you," our son says a little hesitantly, inspecting the brand new phone. His little sister, quick as a flash, has got hold of the box and its colourful wrapping and wants to play with it. "And there is something else," I announce proudly. Jordan puts the mobile down and frowns. "What?" he asks. "I'm going to move back home tonight," I inform him happily. "Oh, Dad. That's great, thank you," Jordan exclaims, moving so awkwardly in his bed that he screams out in pain straight afterwards. My eyes are meeting Angie's. She's still unsure but even if she is doing it for Jordan we are making progress.

Angie, Melanie and I are having our evening meal at the hospital, and then I leave to take my daughter home to Launceston before Barbara and Charles arrive to visit Jordan. Feeling happy and relieved I stop over at the Travelodge to pack my bags and check out. It is a gorgeous evening. The thought of soon being on the road home, moving my few belongings back into our house, settling back and sleeping in our own bed tonight, really excites me. Carrying Melanie in my arms I go to my room. I put Melanie on the bed and switch my phone back on: Time to look at all those messages that I have not read, time to delete all the missed calls from Beth.

Suddenly I hesitate. It is no good just ignoring her calls. I must ring her and tell her that it is over, once and for all. I must apologise to her, thank her but I don't even get a chance to think any further about what to say or what to do. The phone rings and the caller is Beth. I should have known better but this time I answer.

"Darling, what's up with you?" Beth greets me. I feel nervous. My heart is pounding heavily in my chest. "I turned my phone off in the hospital," I reply immediately, hoping my courage is not going to fail me. "I've been trying to tell you all day long that I've decided to delay my trip back to Surrey. After breakfast I bought the local newspaper and I saw an advert for a flat. It was too good to miss. So I've spent the day sorting our future accommodation out," Beth tells me proudly. "I must tell you all about it." I just manage to stop Melanie from falling off the bed as I take a long deep breath. "It's overlooking the Tamar, an easy drive to work

123

for you, in a brand-new building, three bedrooms..," Beth continues but I interrupt: "Hang on, Beth. I am about to move back to Launceston," I say quickly. My hands are shaking, my voice is croaky but I have made a start. "You are what?" Beth asks. "I'm sorry, Beth but Angie and I have decided to give our marriage another chance," I respond truthfully. My words make Beth laugh. "So you've told her about us, what we've done in your cottage when you should have been playing golf – and she has forgiven you, just like this?" she wants to know. "It's none of your business, Beth," I snap angrily. "Oh, yes, it is. If you haven't told her, then I will. What kind of reconciliation is this? You've been unfaithful, you've lied to her. That's no basis to rebuild a marriage on!" Beth shouts at me. "Please, Beth. Your boys have almost grown up but we have to think about our children," I try to explain. "The children! What about me? I've left my husband for you because I can't live with all those lies. I want to be with you. For me it was not a quick, meaningless affair. I am not giving you up this easily, Rob," Beth confirms. "I bet you haven't even told your wife that it was me who drove you to the hospital and back last night! I guess you've told her that your driver was a man, am I right? Tell her the truth, Rob. If she is still prepared to have a relationship with you after all that, then I will accept it."

I am feeling bullied again, so much so that I say: "No, you have no right to tell me what to do. What we had must end here and now. I'm sorry, Beth. It was a big mistake. Please understand." With that I end the call and take Melanie into my arms.

My little daughter senses that something is wrong and she starts crying. I hug her tenderly. "It's not your fault, darling. Everything will be alright," I tell her but I don't believe a word I say. Nothing will be alright, nothing at all. Looking at the digital clock on the Travelodge's television set I realise that it is time for Melanie to go to bed. Despite it all I must get on with packing my bags. Much later than I intended I finally check out of my room and drive back to Launceston.

Again using Angie's new keys I let myself into our house. Before doing anything else I try to concentrate on Melanie. She is overtired and in need of a good night's sleep. All the upheaval has made her rather unsettled. I have already spent more than an hour in her room, trying to calm her down when my phone rings. I know immediately that it is safe to answer this call. "Justin" it reads on the display. "Finally! I've been trying to ring you all day," my best friend complains. "They told me at your garage that Jordan is in hospital but every time I tried your mobile it was switched off. I'm glad that I've eventually got hold of you. Tell me exactly what happened!" Justin demands. Keeping a close eye on my young daughter I tell Justin what I know about Jordan's accident. My dear friend listens carefully. "Poor boy," he comments and then he offers: "Obviously, we are a little far away but if there is anything we can do to help we will." "Thanks," I reply lamely. When he asks me how I am I pretend that I am coping fine.

After I've finished the conversation with Justin I go to the kitchen. There is no beer in the house and little alcohol besides. Will Beth really have the nerve to tell Angie about our affair? How would she go about it? Am I worrying unnecessarily or is my only chance to come clean with Angie before Beth does? I don't know what to do. Earlier

125

today I thought my marriage is slowly getting back on track and tonight, here I am in the worst position ever.

Although I am pleased to be back in our own comfortable bed I cannot sleep. Melanie has me up twice which does not help either. When the alarm goes off at 7 am I feel totally shattered. Trying hard to get Beth out of my mind, I dress and feed Melanie, but I don't have time to have breakfast myself. Skipping breakfast yet again I set off towards Plymouth.

Jordan is feeling a lot better this morning. The nurses have got him out of bed early and shown him how to use crutches. Angie tells me that she has had a much better night, too. "All being well Jordan will be able to come home with us today. We are just waiting for the consultant to come around and check that he will be OK to leave this afternoon," she reports happily. "I've been out in the corridor talking to Tom on my mobile. He'll be coming to see me at home this evening," Jordan says cheerfully. Angie holds Melanie's small hand, walking around the ward with her. "In that case I may be able to take Mum out for a nice meal tonight," I reply, watching my wife and daughter. "Yeah, sure. There will be plenty of people around – Tom, Justin and Judy," Jordan agrees. "We'll have to take Melanie with us though," Angie says, not smiling.

Just before lunch the consultant confirms that Jordan will be able to go home this afternoon. He promises to get the necessary paperwork ready for us and everyone is very pleased. While Jordan is having his lunch on the ward Angie, Melanie and I decide to have a quick bite in the cafeteria. Then we make our way home with Jordan in the passenger seat next me so that he can stretch his injured leg out.

Justin, Judy and Tom arrive at 6pm. To my absolute surprise Judy is offering to look after Melanie for a couple of hours which means that I can go ahead with my plans to take Angie out for a meal. I am determined to spend some "adult only" time with her over dinner. Deep inside I feel anxious though. Here is an opportunity for us to have a serious talk. I must make the most of it. In happier days we used to frequent a small restaurant serving French food. We have not been there since Jordan was born, I don't think. I don't even know if it still exists.

With Angie by my side I drive off. If I am hoping for some friendly conversation I will be disappointed. Angie looks out of the passenger side window saying nothing. It is hard to come up with a suitable topic but I ask her if she can remember our favourite restaurant. "We've only got a couple of hours, Rob. No need to spend that kind of money on food either," she says slowly. There is not even a hint of enthusiasm in her voice. The expression on her face tells me that she would rather not have dinner with me tonight. Without a reservation there is no space for us in the few local restaurants so we end up in the pub, the White Horse Inn, which is the one closest to my current work place. "Take your phone in with you, Rob, just in case Judy has trouble with Melly. We mustn't be too late getting back," Angie says urgently. She seems on edge but I obediently put my mobile in my pocket.

The light summer's evening is warm enough for us to sit outside. We share a picnic bench under an enormous old tree. Angie orders a large glass of red wine and I am having a lovely cold pint of lager. We sit opposite each other, behaving like strangers. "I'm glad that you will be able to go back to work tomorrow. Presumably you've had to take leave," my wife says, concentrating on watching sparrows picking up crumbs under our table rather than looking at me. "It's not a big deal. I'll probably have a few days holiday owed to me. Once I've had my leaving party it will be all over anyway," I reply casually. Then I add: "I'm going to miss Launceston." "It was your decision to move on. Don't ever forget that," Angie reminds me. "I know. We'll get used to it, I'm sure," I reply, taking her hand. I wish I could get closer to her but somehow I sense that Angie is not ready for too much physical contact with me yet.

Soon I go inside the cosy historic pub to order our food. The wind has picked up considerably so we decide to have our meal indoors. All Angie wants to talk about over dinner is our divorce. I don't want to hear of it. After a while I make my excuses and go to the "gents". This evening has not turned out the way I would have hoped. It is going to be tough to regain Angie's trust. When I return to our table I say to her: "I'd like you to come to my leaving party, please." Angie shakes her head. "I am sorry, Rob but I did not want you to leave and I don't want to be there when people are asking questions. Please save me from having to make up stories and pretend that I am happy about your move. You know that I am not keen on these office parties anyway." With that she looks at her watch. "We should be heading back," she says shifting nervously in her chair.

During the next couple of days the temptation to ring Beth is tearing me up inside. I want to apologise to her for finishing our relationship over the telephone. I want to explain myself to her but I have resolved that I must let matters rest. I am not going to risk losing the tiny amount of progress I have made with Angie. As hard as it seems, I must learn to stay away from danger.

I still think of Beth though, by far too much, but I keep ignoring her calls and messages. At night when I am in my lonely bed I am secretly hoping that maybe she has returned to Brian. Perhaps he has been able to forgive her for one short fling and everything will continue as before but then again, I am not sure if that is possible. Although Angie and I live under the same roof again our relationship remains rather strained. My wife is not prepared to let me use our double bed any longer so it is me who currently resides on the guest bed in Melanie's room. We are not quarrelling anymore but our marriage has not returned to normal yet. I know I will have to be patient.

Finally, the day of my dreaded leaving party has arrived. With Angie and my children refusing to attend I am not looking forward to the evening at all. During the day I am busy clearing everything that belongs to me out of my office. I must admit that it hurts immensely. I have liked it here. It is tough to say farewell to a job you've loved, particularly as my future still seems so uncertain at present.

If only this party could be a low-key, quick affair! Judging by the amount of well-dressed people who arrive at the showroom tonight Jackie must have advertised the event as this year's biggest social gathering in North Cornwall. All our shiny brand new cars have been moved to a safe area behind the workshop and the showroom has been transformed into a large party hall with plenty of space for eating, drinking and dancing. I feel moved, humbled and a little embarrassed by it all. The amount of hugs and kisses I receive in the space of fifteen minutes is quite overwhelming, terrifying in fact. If only my family were here tonight to support me but Angie has made it very clear why she does not want to attend, and also, I think that she has actually never cared for my colleagues at the dealership too much anyway. I have to accept that she is not prepared to do me any favours at the moment.

One of my colleagues who works in our servicing department is the guitarist in a local band. He has brought his friends along and they are playing their songs especially for me. I should be thankful and feel honoured but I hate all this fuss. It makes me uncomfortable. Somehow I feel vulnerable. After all, I am the main character here – and I am supposed to look confident. Alcohol is definitely not the answer. Whatever it takes, I must stay calm and in control. It won't be long until the firm's director will say a few words about me and my time at the company, and maybe Jackie as well. All the guests will expect me to deliver a sensible reply. I am trying to go easy on the bubbly but, of course, everyone wants to have a drink with me. Too much booze is bound to affect my head. I watch in trepidation as more and more people are pouring into the showroom. I must either have been very popular or the whole town has been invited to make up numbers.

We are lucky with the weather, too. This evening has turned out extremely well. It is sunny and warm. Guests are able to spread out into the forecourt. *Please, Lord, let this party be over soon. I don't want it. It makes me want to cry. I want my old life back. Let's wipe out the last three months. Let's pretend all this is not really happening.* All kinds of thoughts are buzzing through my brain.

Soon I find myself chatting to our workshop manager who has partnered me in a couple of golf tournaments during my time here. Then we hear the sound of the bell at the make-shift bar. "Ladies and gentlemen," announces the still very forceful voice of our aging director. Here we go, the formal part of the evening is about to start. It has suddenly gone very quiet around the showroom and outside. Attentively everyone is listening to the director's speech. So many good things are being said about me! I have not deserved it. Anyone who knows my private life has to concede that I am not the "goodie-goodie" that people make me out to be. I am thinking of Angie and Jordan who can confirm that I am a horrible man who is telling lies and doing things behind their backs, letting his family and himself down. At this moment I wish I had the nerve to confess all of my sins, ask for forgiveness but all I do is put on a fake smile and pretend to be happy.

Blinded by the huge amount of flash lights from various cameras that guests are using to get one final picture of me I take a step to one side. Then I am presented with an enormous gift. The gathered crowd urges me to unwrap it. Out of the beautifully soft paper comes a fantastic painting of the North Cornish coast, all expertly framed and finished off with a shiny brass plate, inscribed especially for me. I am stunned, totally gobsmacked. The amount of generosity and kindness shown to me this evening is quite incredible. Proudly I hold the picture aloft, almost collapsing under the sheer weight of it. My hands shaking I put the present down again. People are clapping when my eyes scan the room. This cannot be true. I must be dreaming. At a safe distance from the applauding crowd I spot a lonely figure. How can a few glasses of sparkling wine cause such delirium? It's not a dream. I recognise the engaging smile on that pretty face at the very far end of the showroom. It hits me in the same way it has done when I saw it for the first time.

It takes my breath away – what on earth is Beth doing here? Who has invited her? All eyes are on me but I dare not show my confusion, my churned up emotions. Clearing my throat I look at Jackie who is standing next to me. It is time for me to say something, something intelligent and show my appreciation. This is all getting too much for me. I start talking, gabbling, don't really know what I am saying, apart from a big thank-you, of course.

As the final applause ceases I take another glance over at Beth. From her corner in the background she is still smiling and nodding encouragingly. This is hard, terribly difficult. I can see that she is proud of me, just like Angie would have been, had she been here. At this point I should have thanked my family for all the support they have given me over the years but not one of them has turned up. Not even my Mum felt up to coming out tonight, and, of course, Angie's parents have not been invited. Politely I thank the company, customers and friends and in particular my dear colleague Jackie who has done so much to make this evening a memorable one.

Luckily this seems sufficient. I don't need to say anymore. The band strikes up and the buffet is declared open. All the formalities of the evening are suddenly over. I don't know what to do. Should I go and greet Beth, ask her why she is here? Should I pretend she is an old friend and introduce her as such or should I just ignore her, hope that she will go away? The director has put my large picture in his office for safe keeping. He passes me my glass and pats me on the shoulder. "We'll miss you, Rob. Good luck in Plymouth," he says kindly. Everyone disperses. For just a second I feel lonely in the noisy crowd. Jackie and her female friend are waving at me but nobody is actually talking to me at this very moment. Less than a minute later any indecision has quickly been taken out of my hands. Beth makes a bee line for me. All of a sudden she is standing right in front of me, looking gorgeous in her elegant red dress and high heels. "Hi," I greet her shyly. The last thing I want is being seen with her so I decide that natural behaviour is the safest way forward in these circumstances. "Hi, well done," she replies, smiling sweetly. Her right hand is reaching out for my tie. "I've never seen you dressed up like this. You look great, very smart," she adds. "Let's have a bite to eat, I'm starving," I invite her, ignoring her remark and leading her to the long buffet table. "What are you doing here?" I whisper angrily as we fill our plates with food. "I've come to see you, what else!" she responds immediately. Then she continues: "You know that I won't give you up without a fight." I decide to take her outside, smiling at my numerous guests as we move along.

"Where's your wife?" Beth enquires, leaning seductively on the bonnet of one of our second-hand cars in the forecourt. "Looking after the children," I snap aggressively. The smile on Beth's beautiful face seems brighter than ever. I remain standing well away, not wanting to attract attention. If only I could take my plate and run, never to return.

It's no use wishing my time away. All I can do is ask Beth to leave me alone and not spoil the party. I don't want her here. "Listen, Beth. I don't want to be seen with you. Not here, not now. Please go home, do me this one favour, please," I plead but she just smiles and walks off to get us another drink. I am not used to this amount of alcohol and I am beginning to feel horribly intoxicated.

As the minutes go by a couple of younger guests start dancing. I cannot remember the last time I have done that. It must have been with Angie but it seems a long time ago. Admittedly I fancy asking Beth to dance but on the other hand I would rather she went home. Her presence irritates me immensely. She does not know anyone here so she is bound to stay by my side, if I like it or not. Reluctantly I introduce her as a "family friend". I find it embarrassing, inappropriate. Although I have not known her for very long I realise that I should never underestimate her ability to change my mind. "I'd love to dance," she tells me in front of the company director and his wife who we have been talking to for the last half hour. There is no way I can turn her down without causing embarrassment so I simply take her to the dance floor and all good intensions go down the drain. "Great party, darling," Beth whispers, putting her slim arms around me. I have had by far too much to drink to resist any longer. All my doubts and negative feelings about her seem to magically disappear as we move to the music. Holding the lovely Beth in my arms I begin to relax, forget the world around me and enjoy myself.

What started as an awfully uncomfortable evening is about to become the best party ever. I cannot remember if I have ever felt this happy before. Beth is wearing me out. We are laughing, dancing, having so much fun. She is such great company and so extremely sexy with it.

Eventually a lot of guests are leaving. Like a robot I say good-night to everyone, using the same words over and over again. I am still having a wonderful time with the vivacious Beth. Hot and totally exhausted from too much activity on the dance floor we walk arm in arm across the forecourt. My car is parked at the back of the long showroom building. I feel unsteady on my feet but I am on cloud nine. I drag Beth to my VW, pull the key out my pocket and unlock the doors. Checking that no one is watching we disappear into the car where I finally get the chance to kiss her, long and passionately, just like I used to in Crantock. "I could not let this day pass without seeing you," she confesses, stroking me tenderly. "I rang the dealership and they told me about your leaving do," she continues. After a moment of silence she asks: "Please, Rob, tell me the truth. You are not seriously considering returning to your wife, are you?"

I pull her over to the driver's side of my car. The consumption of too much alcohol has made my speech slurry. I am fighting to string the words together, struggling to express myself clearly. "I have to, please understand, I...," is all I can say before my fingers make their way to the many fiddly buttons that fasten Beth's lovely summer dress. I am about to lose my last resolve. I give up, give in, don't care anymore. Given half a chance I would make love to her right here but thankfully she is in much better condition than I am. "Stop, Rob, behave yourself!" I hear her say. "Let's call a taxi. We'll go to my hotel," she suggests quickly. "Hotel," that's the word that makes me sit up straight. *I must go home*, voices in my head are telling me. It is pitch dark around us. The windows of my car have steamed up completely. I feel disorientated and sick. Then I realise that Beth is shivering so I put my warm arms firmly around her. We get out of the car, staggering back across the forecourt. I am embarrassingly unsteady. "Pull yourself together, darling!" Beth advises as we approach the entrance to the showroom. Smiling she lets me collapse into one of the wide leather tub chairs by the door while she goes off to order the cab.

Sitting, well almost lying, in the chair I am trying to gather my thoughts. I am half asleep, feeling a little woozy. There is hardly anyone around apart from the catering staff who are clearing up. My hands are holding on to the cool leather of the comfortable chair for dear life. Everything is spinning around in circles, not a great sensation. "Come on. You look as if you could do with some fresh air. The taxi will be here in a minute," I hear Beth say. She is taking my hand and pulls me outside. In silence we are walking, in my case swaying, to the end of the wide drive that leads from the dealership to the main road. As I see a pair of strong headlights approaching I make a reasonably conscious decision not to spend the night with Beth. It's not that I don't want her but I am just feeling too rough to be a good lover. I need a bed, on my own, as soon as possible.

Beth is starting to look a little concerned about my condition. She pushes me into the taxi and tells the driver where to go but last minutes I regain enough will power to disagree with the suggested route. As clearly as I can I tell the driver my home address and I insist to be taken there first. Within seconds Beth and I start arguing until the driver gets angry. Stamping some authority onto the matter he threatens not to take us anywhere if we can't agree on the destination. Taking a deep breath I sit up in my seat and make sure he has understood me correctly – first my home in Launceston, then Beth's hotel on the outskirts. As the car starts moving off I am holding Beth's hand. She does not look very happy now and I am fighting both tiredness and nausea.

I have no idea what the time is when the taxi drops me off outside my house. I stagger to the front door, not even waving Beth farewell. Needless to say I have a hard job to find my key. I can still hear the diesel engine of the cab rattling away at the top of our drive but I am determined to succeed in my attempts to get entry to my home. Eventually I pull the key out of my trouser pocket. I even manage to fit it straight into the lock. With a sigh of relief I let myself into the dark and quiet house.

I am surprising myself by walking up the stairs quite steadily. The door to Melanie's room is slightly ajar. On tiptoes I creep inside, taking a quick look at my baby. She is sleeping peacefully. I get undressed and make my way to the bathroom. This is when Angie catches up with me. "Where have you been? Surely your leaving do did not go on until after midnight?" she asks, her hands on her hips. "You've missed a brilliant party," I respond, deliberately not answering her question. "I can see that. You can hardly stand up!" Angie points out while watching me hold on to our hand basin. I want to say something to her but I am not up to it at the moment. "Please don't wake Melanie up," is all Angie says. Then she leaves me to my own devices.

It is the sound of my mobile phone that wakes me up later that morning. Slightly confused I am searching the pockets of my trousers that I have dumped carelessly on the floor next to the guest bed. By the time I eventually get to my phone it has finished ringing. My head is buzzing but it takes me only seconds to realise that it was Beth who has been trying to reach me. She has left a voicemail message so I get up and walk over to the cot to see if Melanie is still sleeping. Her cot is empty. Presumably Angie has got her up while I was still away with the fairies.

Leaning onto the empty cot I listen to Beth's voice. "Hope you are OK, darling. I'm on my way back to Surrey – urgent business. Talk to you later. Love you. Lots of kisses." Sighing I delete the message. I need a shower and a dose of strong pain killers. When I eventually go down for breakfast I find that only Jordan is home. "Where's Mum?" I ask him. "She's got an appointment or something," he tells me. I am surprised that she has taken Melanie with her but I don't want to discuss this with my son. "How do you feel about a little trip, just you and me?" I ask him. "Where will we be going? I can't walk much like this," Jordan replies, pointing at his colourful plaster cast. "That's OK. Where we are going you don't need to walk at all," I say, struggling to finish my bowl of cereal. Jordan does not look too enthusiastic but at least he agrees to come with me.

First of all we are taking a taxi back to the car dealer's where I have left my car last night. I need to pick up my wonderful leaving present. Also, I need to make arrangements for the hand-over of all keys and agree a date and time for the return of my current company car. Entering the premises gives me goose pimples. This may well be the last time for quite a while that I shall set foot on the place that has meant more than just work for me. I try not to show any mixed emotions in front of Jordan but I have to admit that I feel a little shaky. Once we've got the picture in the car and I have completed the necessary paperwork for the return of the car I say my last good-byes to everyone. Then we drive off. I am telling my son about the cottage that I have inherited. "I'd like to show it to you," I say but Jordan does not seem to be too interested. He is in a strange mood, not quite himself at all. I have rarely seen him with such a grim expression on his young face.

On the way to Crantock we are not talking much. It is a most unpleasant journey. I am still feeling hung over and apart from anything else it has started to rain. More and more grey clouds are building up in the sky above us. As I am driving along I am keeping an eye on my son next to me. He looks unhappy and bored, playing with his mobile phone like a teenager.

Around 2pm we reach the pub in Crantock, just before the kitchen closes. With it being the end of the school holidays and the weather so poor the Old Albion is extremely busy. We are lucky to get a table. Jordan's agitated mood changes slightly once he has food in his stomach but he is still not prepared to say very much. If I ask him a straight question he will answer. I just cannot engage him in any meaningful conversation. "We'll go to my cottage now," I tell him once I have settled the bill. It is still raining heavily outside. We get back into the car and I drive the short distance to my property.

Jordan is not impressed. Not only is the garden in desperate need of attention again but the old house feels typically cold and damp as we enter. Nothing is quite like I remember it either. The letting agency's cleaners have re-arranged the furniture and drawn all the curtains. I can't help thinking of Beth, recalling the wonderful time we've experienced here. "It's horrible, Dad. Surely, you are not going to keep this," Jordan remarks as he limps around the small lounge. I inspect the walls, knock on the ceiling and assess the corners for damp spots. "With a little bit of work it can be transformed into a very valuable home," I explain to my son. "I don't like it. Can we go now?" Jordan asks impatiently. "But you've not seen upstairs yet. I'll give you a hand," I offer immediately. "I don't want to see it. I want to do something fun," Jordan states decisively. I am upstairs now checking the rooms out. "Once we've finished here I'll take you to Newquay. You may find it more exciting there," I suggest, trying to persuade Jordan to stay a little longer. Still refusing to join me upstairs Jordan sits at the bottom of the stairs while I ensure that all rooms in the cottage are clean and tidy.

"Oh, sh..!" I can just about stop myself but my aborted swearword makes my son pay attention. "What is it, Dad?" he shouts up to me. I have found a bad leak in the ceiling of the second bedroom which forces me to explore the roof space. "I'll have go and see the neighbour. Hopefully he will have a long ladder in his shed," I tell Jordan. Before I leave the cottage I also advise him that we may well have to stay for another hour yet.

In the pouring rain I knock onto the neighbour's door. He is the one who helped Beth with the burst water pipe. A little reluctantly he agrees to come over to assess the newly found damage with me. Ladder across his shoulder he follows me next door. "This is my son Jordan," I introduce the miserable looking youngster at the bottom of the small staircase. Politely my boy shakes the neighbour's large hand. "You haven't fallen off one of these, have you?" the neighbour who introduces himself as George, asks, looking at Jordan's bright blue plaster cast and carrying the ladder up the stairs. "No, football," Jordan replies, not smiling. "Well, let's take a look at your roof then," George suggests kindly, following me to the trap door in the ceiling of the landing. He climbs up into the tight roof space, instructing me to hold the ladder for him. Jordan is leaning on his crutches now, looking up to where George is working.

"Good Lord! Have you ever been up here?" I hear George's deep voice shout from above. "No," I reply truthfully, feeling a little embarrassed. "Bit of a treasure trove, I must say... Ah, I can see it, I think, I've found the leak!" George reports proudly. "Anything you can do to fix it?" I ask him. "Yes, I hope so. I'll have to get my tools though," he responds quickly. Jordan has overheard the word "treasure" and now he is keen to visit upstairs after all.

While George is next door fetching the necessary equipment to at least temporarily fix my roof I help Jordan up the narrow stairs. "What is up there so much, Dad?" my son asks. With him holding on to the ladder I climb up to take a look for myself. Fortunately George has left his torch up here so I can see what he means. There are heaps of ancient, dust-covered photograph albums, cases containing silver cutlery, a leather suitcase full of old-fashioned clothes and shoes, a box filled with jewellery and to my great surprise a lovely old golf bag with a set of rusty clubs and a wooden tennis racket with broken strings. "I'm surprised the letting agent has not told me about all this," I remark. "We must get the stuff down and have a proper look at it," Jordan suggests eagerly. He is struggling to see anything at all from where he is standing. "Yes, I agree but we won't have time to do that today," I refuse. "Please, Dad, just one of the albums perhaps," Jordan demands. Dusting the top album off with my bare hand I take a quick look myself before passing it down to Jordan. "Gran may recognise some people in those photos," I say when I eventually give the old album to my son.

When George returns Jordan is sitting on the single bed in bedroom number two examining the fascinating pictures. I simply hold the ladder, unable to assist George any further with the repairs to the roof. "To be honest I cannot see this lasting the winter. The cottage needs a new roof," George tells me while he is working. He points out to me where wind and rain will soon start to attack the cracks. "I can tell you, as nice as they are, old properties eat up your money faster than you can earn it," he warns me. "I am hoping to sell," I explain. "Won't get this one through the survey though, not in this state," is George's immediate reaction. "Unless you do it up you won't get much for it. Nobody will buy a place like this," my neighbour argues. I am tempted to tell him that I've had one very good offer already but then I decide that I do not wish to go into any details.

Jordan is desperate to look at more photos so I get George to pass another couple of albums down. Eventually my kind neighbour has done the necessary to prevent the rain from penetrating the dodgy roof. I offer to pay him but he refuses. "Your last tenant has been very generous when I fixed the pipes. I couldn't possibly accept any more from you. This was only a small job," George explains. Smiling he climbs down the ladder, then helps me to close the precarious looking flap that leads to the roof space. I see him and his long ladder off while Jordan is completely engrossed in viewing the many stunning black and white photographs and the neatly written captions.

"Looks like your auntie was very sporty, Dad," Jordan remarks. We recognise the golf bag in the photos and there are also pictures of a well-built lady in tennis dress, lifting a beautiful trophy. "Can we take these home, please, Dad?" Jordan asks, holding on to the albums. "Yes, why not - but you will have to be very careful with them," I agree. Then I go in search of a plastic bag and find one in the kitchen. With some difficulties Jordan limps down the narrow stairs and back into the car.

The rain has stopped. I would have liked to show my son the wonderful beach but in his present condition he will not be able to walk up the steep dunes anyway. Clutching the treasured photograph albums he is sitting in the back seat, no longer bothered if we are going to do "something fun" or not.

On the way back to Launceston I ignore several calls and messages from Beth. I am glad that she is back in Surrey for a while. Not having given in too much to her seductive ways and my decision not to go back to the hotel with her last night makes me feel quite proud of myself. From now on I will try to stay away from her. It will be tough but I am going to give my last chance of the reconciliation with Angie my best shot.

When we arrive home Jordan takes the bag with the photograph albums straight to the kitchen where Angie is feeding Melanie. "Look, Mum, look what we have found!" he exclaims excitedly. Angie looks pale, strained, almost as if she has been crying. She completely ignores her enthusiastic son's request. "I would like you to go upstairs for a little while, Jordan," she tells him rather formally. The happy smile on our boy's face disappears instantly. "Ok," he agrees immediately, taking the old albums with him when leaving the kitchen. In the middle of our kitchen table is Angie's laptop, the lid closed but as soon as I approach she opens it up. "Talking about photographs…," she says to me, fighting tears. Filling the entire screen in front of me is a good-quality shot of me and Beth dancing closely at last evening's party. This particular photograph shows Beth's lips kissing my neck. "There are more," Angie continues. At the push of one button she calls up a whole series of photographs, all showing me and Beth. There is even a pretty clear one of my car, steamy windows and all. I am shaking, trying hard to keep my composure. "Who has sent them?" I ask, dropping into one of our kitchen chairs. "That does not matter. I want to know why Beth Henderson was at your leaving party – without her husband!" Angie says firmly. "They were both invited. He is away on business. I'm sorry, I got a little carried away yesterday. I had too much to drink," I explain helplessly. Angie shakes her head. "Stop telling lies, Rob. Neither Beth nor Brian Henderson was officially invited. I have spoken to Jackie. Beth Henderson must have been your personal guest." This is where Angie has to stop. She breaks down in tears, unable to put into words what she must be feeling right now.

Taking a deep breath I bow my head. It is time for me to come clean, finally tell the truth. I cannot and will not deny it any longer. "I'm so sorry, Angie," I whisper, ready to go into further detail about my affair with Beth but Angie turns away. Drying her eyes with a tea towel she nods. "I want you to leave the house, Rob – for good this time. Our divorce will be going ahead and I shall not change my mind. If you have any respect left for me or the children then let us get on with life as soon as possible. Please don't cause any more upset," she tells me. With that she closes the lid of the laptop, picks it up, lifts Melanie out of her highchair and storms out of the kitchen.

So this is it – a couple of party pictures bringing an end to my marriage, just like that. I am ashamed of myself, feeling such a fool. I hate myself and Beth for what we have done. Deep down I wonder if she has anything to do with the photographs. Maybe I will never know. Very slowly I get up from my chair. There is nothing more I can do, nothing more I can say. It's all my own doing, my own fault. I decide that I must talk to Jordan before I leave. He is still young but he has a right to know what is going on. My head spinning I walk upstairs towards his room. Unsure how to convey the truth I approach the door. I can hear voices from inside the room. Angie has beaten me to it. Listening carefully, ear to the door like a nosy child, I try to pick up snippets of the conversation. For minutes I stand there, on the landing, outside of Jordan's door, eavesdropping. I must not be caught, I must pack my bags, yet again. Sighing I turn away, just in time not to embarrass myself any further.

Much quicker than ever before, I throw my few belongings back into a large holdall. Angie has left Jordan's room. She is taking Melanie to bed. My throat feels awfully dry, I wish I could be given the opportunity to explain myself but what difference would it make? Angie does not want to hear how I got involved with Beth, that I fell for her like I have never fallen for anyone before, but that it is all over now. She would never believe me and I can't blame her. I have betrayed her trust and this is the price I have to pay for my infidelity.

As I take my briefcase in readiness to go to my car Jordan catches up with me. "Dad!" he shouts after me. I turn around, feeling weak and endlessly sad. On his crutches my little boy looks so fragile. "Dad, where are you going?" he asks me, tears in his eyes. "I don't know," I reply and that is actually true. "I'll be in Plymouth from Monday onwards," I add then. Jordan nods but he is lacking understanding. Having put my luggage into the boot I step forward to take my son into my arms. "I'll keep in touch and I'll see you and Melly as often as I can. That's a promise," I say firmly and kiss him. With that I send him back into the house and drive off at high speed.

I get as far as the petrol station on the main road before I have to stop. Resting my aching head on the steering wheel I break down and cry. Yes, a fully grown middle-aged man, sitting in his car, parked up outside the car wash, crying like a little baby. Looking at my hands I realise that it is time for me to remove my wedding ring but I have difficulties pulling it off. Eventually, after suffering considerable pain, I manage to make it budge. Wiping my eyes I drop it into the console by the gear stick. The ugly white mark that the missing ring has left on my tanned finger brings a fleeting smile to my sad face. Then I try to compose myself and re-start the engine. Pretending to be strong I turn the car around, heading towards the petrol pumps. Rather than returning to the Travelodge in Plymouth I decide to spend the night in my cottage in Crantock.

All of a sudden I look forward to the drive, the idea of getting away, on my own. So I fill the tank, go to pay, pick up a couple of essentials in the petrol station's well stocked shop and off I go. With my mobile phone switched off I remain undisturbed until I get to my destination.

Once I've parked the car, have let myself into the cottage, pulled back the curtains and opened all the windows to air the place, I stroll down to the beach. It is almost dark now but the view over the dunes is still fabulous. Above me the sky appears purple-grey, such an amazing colour created by the pale light of a full moon. Sand in my shoes I walk towards the water's edge. A keen late summer night's breeze is ruffling my hair. The strong wind, down by the sea, makes me shiver. This is the most romantic location and I cannot deny that I am missing Beth. Being with her has been a fantastic experience but I am not convinced that I really love her. Aimlessly I wander along the wide beach, feeling very emotional. It is the sound of the tide rolling in that brings back memories. Wondering what the future may hold for me I walk back towards the high dunes. The picture of Brian Henderson standing at the top, watching me kiss his attractive wife will never completely disappear from my mind. How could I ever forget this horrible feeling of being found out? I shall sell the cottage and avoid coming here ever again.

At pace I stride towards the pub, just before closing time. The few people who are left in the bar assess me curiously. I don't fit in, don't belong here. I am clearly not one of the locals and I will probably never be. Drinking my pint I am feeling extremely uncomfortable, strangely self-conscious, among the regulars. Uneasily I empty my glass and escape. I am almost jogging back to the cottage. My confidence has taken a knock, not a great prospect for starting a new job.

Once back in the cottage I turn my mobile back on. A barrage of messages is coming in as I walk up the stairs to the large bedroom that I've shared with Beth. My cold fingers scroll through the texts. Justin, bless him, has entered us for a tournament and wants my entry fee, Jordan wishes me a good night, Beth says that she loves me and wants me to ring her, Jackie hopes I'll enjoy my new job and wishes me luck – everyone is so kind but all I wish for is a message from Angie saying: *Please come home, I want us to be a normal family again. I will forgive you if you promise*…forget it, it is never going to happen. Slowly I sit down on the unmade bed. I feel lonely. Nothing would be easier than getting in touch with Beth but I have finally resolved not to.

Luckily I find some bed linen in one of the wardrobes. The sheets feel slightly damp, emanating a mouldy odour but they will have to do. Yawning I make my bed. I will have to learn to do a lot more for myself when I live in Plymouth. Once I have closed the curtains I put the small radio on that I've found in the kitchen. Although I am tired I cannot go to sleep. Lying in my cold bed, listening to soothing late night music, I wonder yet again who might have taken the photographs at my leaving party and who is responsible for sending them on to Angie. I know that Beth has been threatening to tell my wife about our affair if I didn't. Tossing and turning in the bed I try to recall if there was anyone around that evening who I did not know. There were so many people and a lot of photographs were taken. What if it was not Beth who has engineered all this? Who else would have an interest in my private life? With nothing but questions on my mind I eventually drift off.

I have a bit of a lie-in on Sunday morning, something I have rarely had since Melanie was born. The sun is shining beautifully, lifting my spirits considerably. I make myself a cup of tea and eat my cereal outside in the garden where the birds are singing. Sitting back on my rather wobbly kitchen chair I remember the fateful morning when I joined Beth for breakfast. In my mind the picture is still so clear, every little detail, the colour of the flowers on the table, Beth's lovely dress, her smile, the way we started flirting, laughing and joking, this incredible stir in my entire body, like a fire burning inside me, lust, desire, an insatiable hunger for sexual adventure. She has revived all kinds of long lost feelings in me and taught me a great number of new ones which only she can satisfy.

I get up to fetch my mobile. Checking the time I decide to ring Justin. I am surprised to hear that he is on the golf course already, practicing. "You'd better find yourself a new partner," I tell him. I am trying to explain that I have hardly played any golf at all lately and that I don't feel up to entering competitions at the moment. It is quite embarrassing to think that at this rate Justin will show me up badly when we next play in a tournament. Although he is a very good friend I don't think he understands what a depressed wreck I am and that competitive golf is currently the last thing on my mind.

Next I am texting Jordan, telling him that I am missing him and Melanie. I am also enquiring how "Mum" is. Then I am deleting all the various messages from Beth. If she keeps on bothering me I will have to change my phone number. Under no circumstances will I weaken again. Looking back, I feel that she has played a considerable part in destroying

151

my marriage. It takes two, of course, but I am determined to blame her as much as myself.

Before heading to the beach I tidy up the cottage. I want to make it presentable enough for any estate agent to view, measure and photograph it. Judging by the large amount of cars passing by I gather that it will be very busy on the beach today. Determined to enjoy myself I pack my bag, make a couple of sandwiches and leave.

It definitely is another gorgeous late summer Sunday morning, incredibly mild and warm. Walking down the straight road that leads to the two beach car parks I meet holiday makers as well as locals, armed with beach balls, buckets and spades, inflatables and picnic baskets, all heading in the same direction as me.

While everyone else is crossing the car park I take the small costal footpath uphill which leads to a large undulating area of grassy, sheltered bays within the high dunes. Now and again I spot couples seeking privacy and shelter in the soft white sand. I pass them with a shy smile, secretly wishing I could be here with Beth. My aim is to try and find somewhere suitable for myself but it is not easy to pick out a place where I can be completely on my own. Eventually I settle for a sandy niche half way down the dunes, overlooking the turquoise sea. Sitting on an old beach towel I am considering my options for the future. Although I have not started my new job yet I am already wondering how long I will stay in Plymouth. I think of going up-country or abroad - but then, it would be difficult to see the children. All kinds of thoughts are going through my head until I decide that I must go for a swim. Without Beth I find it much harder to jump into the rolling waves. Feeling like a proper chicken I slowly move forward, the clear, icy water touching my knees, then my thighs and when it comes up to my navel I start to shiver. Under the watchful eyes of the lifeguards I eventually submerge my whole body but I have to admit that I find the water pretty cold today. Fighting a couple of breakers I swim out to sea, trying to appear hardy. This is nothing like as wonderful and exciting as it was with Beth. Nothing is quite the same.

After a few minutes I have enough. As fast as I can I leave the water, run across the wide beach and up to my little camp in the dunes. The old towel around my shoulders I realise that I am not enjoying myself at all. Quickly I pack my bag and make my way back to the footpath. I am still freezing although it is nearly noon and a rather warm day. Not even touching my lunch I return to the cottage, draw all the curtains again, fetch my holdall, throw my belongings into the boot of my car, lock up and drive off towards Plymouth.

Instead of going back to the Travelodge I book myself into a traditional bed and breakfast establishment on the main road, only minutes away from my new work place. The pleasant guesthouse owner even offers to cook dinner for me each night if I pay. She shows me to my room which is located right under the roof and therefore extremely hot. Once I've hung up my clothes I am in urgent need of some fresh air. All I want is a short stroll around the block but curiosity is getting the better of me so I make my way to the Mercedes dealership where I will be working from tomorrow onwards. Trying to familiarise myself with the building I wander around the car park before pressing my nose against the massive windows of the modern showroom. I admire the lovely new cars inside, the clean tiled floor, but my heart feels empty. I am not looking forward to tomorrow, in fact I am dreading it.

Anyone who has ever changed their employer will understand what I am going through this first morning. Although I am generally considering myself as a fairly confident person I feel quite nervous. It is not until the Managing Director introduces me to everyone as the new Head of New Car Sales that I realise what this actually means. I am supposed to be the new boss for Sales Representative Will and Sales Trainee Theo. Apart from that I have access to a secretary called Jenny and a Marketing Assistant by the name of Gill. The used-car sales team is also under my control. They are mature Sales Rep John and the slightly younger Ben.

It dawns on me early in the day that I will spend most of my time in the office, preparing sales figures, working on marketing campaigns in order to attract new business and reporting to Head Office. The days of meeting customers in the showroom and going out for test drives with them are well and truly over. All actual sales will be conducted by my staff. I am just there to co-ordinate it all and to ensure that we meet our targets.

The Managing Director takes me around the premises. Then I shake numerous hands before settling down at my brand-new desk. Will has offered to show me the firm's computer system. He has pulled his chair close to mine and starts to introduce me to the unfamiliar technology. I can sense that he has noticed the white mark where my wedding ring used to be on my left ring-finger but I am hoping he will think I have just forgotten to wear my ring this morning. We make good progress until the phone rings. Trainee Theo answers the call immediately.

"Rob, it's for you," he says. Somewhat surprised I take the call. "Hi, how's your first day?" I hear a female voice ask me. How dare Beth ring me at work? "It's fine but I haven't got time to talk," I reply angrily. I can see Theo watching me. The expression on his immaculate face makes it quite clear that he does not think much of the fact that I receive private calls. Why should I worry? I am his boss – but still, I feel very annoyed. Without saying anything more to Beth I end the unwanted conversation and put the phone down. I apologise to Will and continue learning.

It is fairly quiet for a Monday but by the end of the day more and more customers enter the showroom. In

Launceston I would be thinking of packing up at this time of day but it appears that the hours in Plymouth will be much longer. While Will is with a customer I try and get to know young Theo a little better. I have only just started my job here but my instinct tells me that Theo does not like me. Summoning him to my office I ask a couple of questions about the company's sales strategy which he is most reluctant to answer. As I speak I can see him staring at my ring-finger. Instantly I feel my blood pressure rising. Self-consciously I pull my hand away and hide it under the desk. Our conversation is dragging along but when Theo tells me about the Mercedes Open Golf Day competitions and I tell him that I used to play professionally the young man's face lights up. Suddenly he gets totally animated. "Really? Wow, then we will finally do better. Everyone here is absolutely useless!" Theo tells me. I smile. "Looks like I will have to practice a bit more in that case," I add. I am pleased to think that I have achieved something. Perhaps that awkward trainee and I will have a decent rapport in the future. He even offers to take me on at his local club, an invitation that I politely decline.

Much later than anticipated I return to my B & B. My head is spinning from all the new information I have been given. At this moment in time I am not sure if I will like it at the Mercedes dealership but I realise that I have to give it a few more weeks to make a fair assessment. My friendly host serves my dinner. I seem to be the only guest requiring food in the evenings. So I sit there on my own eating, drinking, missing my family and feeling truly sorry for myself. Now and again I look at my mobile but there is nothing from Jordan or Angie. When the phone eventually rings it is Harry, the Managing Director of my new work place. "How did you enjoy today, Rob?" he asks me. We are having a light-hearted conversation until Harry gets to the point: "I understand you haven't got a fixed abode yet, "he starts and continues: "I have a lovely comfortable flat at the County Club in Saltash, just across the Tamar Bridge in Cornwall. We have had tenants in over the summer but from now on the apartment is empty. You will like it – popular golf course, swimming pool, games room etc etc. I am going to make you an offer that you can't resist!" *Oh dear, not another one of those*, I am thinking but I don't say anything. "I'll show you around tomorrow evening, if you like. It'll be perfect for you until you move your family here." Oops, that hurts. I will not "move my family here" as Harry calls it but again, I keep quiet. "Thank you. Yes, I'd like to have a look," I confirm without the slightest amount of enthusiasm in my voice.

Ending the call I wonder if I should phone Beth. The story behind those party photos still bothers me. I want to ask her if she had anything to do with them, and I also want to explain to her why I cannot continue with our relationship. Several times I pick up my mobile from the table and put it down again. Eventually I decide not to call. Back in my small room in the loft, the window wide open, listening to the never-ending traffic noise on the main road below, I feel restless. I get up and sit down, up and down, over and over again, a useless wreck, lonely and unhappy. I prepare a text to Jordan, sending my love to his Mum and Melanie as well. Once I have pressed the send-button I can only wait for a reply. When it does not come I take my jacket and leave the room.

Aimlessly I wander along the pavements of this busy and unattractive part of Plymouth. Trying to escape the constant exhaust fumes I end up in the pub below the Travelodge where I used to reside not so long ago. I order a beer and retreat into a quiet corner. In here I am a complete stranger, a fact that is partly comforting and partly depressing. Another couple of beers later I feel drowsy and decide that I must return to my hot and stuffy B & B.

The next morning turns out to be quite exciting. Just after 9am my new company car arrives at the showroom. It is an estate car, "ideal for the family" as Harry describes it. Our firm is advertised in large letters on each side of the shiny vehicle. The colour is a very sparkly purplish grey, an unusual colour for a Mercedes. It is a beautiful car, with comfortable black leather seats, all the mod cons and offering plenty of space. Compared to my previous car, a mid-range VW, this is pure luxury. Accompanied by Harry I play with the controls, move the driver's seat into the correct position and adjust the mirrors – electronically, of course. Harry walks around the car to inspect it. When he is satisfied with the car's perfect condition he says: "All yours!" and shakes my hand as if I were a customer.

I park my new wheels in the large car park outside the dealership and return to my desk. Luckily I am starting to get to grips with the computer and the huge amount of paperwork I need to produce each day. The job is beginning to get more interesting but I am still under the impressing that neither Will nor Theo will be too keen to support their new boss. Harry allows me to leave work early so I can see his flat in Saltash. We go in his car, another company vehicle, a cabriolet, similar to Beth's. I have to make polite conversation on the way across the Tamar Bridge. Harry asks me about my family. This is tough as I have to admit that I am in the process of getting divorced. From that moment onward there is an awkward silence in the car. I wonder why it is such a stigma. Millions of people are divorcing each year. Why does it appear to be such a problem for Harry?

Thankfully we soon reach the Country Club. Harry has his own parking space which will be mine if I accept his offer. We enter a modern building. Climbing up a short flight of stairs we arrive at "Harry's Place". The flat is certainly attractive. It has wonderful views across the golf course and the interior is as luxurious as the car we have arrived in. I have to say, the entire club almost smells of money.

"Everything on site is free for the owners and I can transfer my club membership to you, of course." Harry says. We stand on the large balcony watching golfers pushing their trolleys below us. "Come on, I'll buy you a drink in the clubhouse and then we will visit the other facilities," Harry offers. It is all too good to be true but I feel nothing but pain inside. My head bowed in sorrow I follow Harry across the car park to the elegant clubhouse. I am in no mood for alcohol but Harry insists. We sit out on the patio, drinking our pints but the conversation remains slow. "You know, I have been thinking of selling the apartment," Harry suddenly says, "but when I see all this I believe it would be madness." I nod silently. "I am going to retire in a couple of years' time and then I will spend all my days here, I think," he continues. I am not interested in his plans but again I nod in agreement. "You look tired, Rob. Perhaps we should make a move and you let me know in the morning if you want to rent the flat or not," Harry says eventually and I am grateful for it. He takes me back to the dealership and drives off.

With a sigh of relief I watch him speed down the road. Very slowly I walk over to my new car, pat the bonnet and leave it in its parking space. It only takes me five minutes to walk back to my temporary accommodation.

I have a dreadful night. It is terribly hot in my room and I am dreaming of Beth. When the alarm goes off on my mobile I wake up bathed in sweat, my heart racing. The phone also indicates that I have received a text message. It is from Jordan and it reads "Miss you Dad xx". The words hurt - if only I could just go home.

Next I am searching the internet for a solicitor. It is about time that I respond to all the correspondence I have received in connection with my divorce. I am particularly interested to hear if I have to share the proceeds from the sale of my cottage in Crantock when the divorce goes through. At the moment it all seems very messy and complicated to me but once I am at work things are looking more positive.

I tell Harry that I will take up his offer. Determined to make progress I then contact a Plymouth legal practice. Will's reserved attitude towards me has not changed much but Theo is virtually eating out of my hands since I have told him about my golfing career. Fortunately I now remember all the names of the other staff including the guys in the workshop. After the initial doubts I believe that I will enjoy working here. My latest plan is to go back to Launceston on Friday afternoon, with Theo driving my new car so that I can take the old VW back to my former employer. I'll then pick up the rest of my personal belongings which includes my golfing equipment, and take Theo back to Plymouth before moving into the Country Club late on Friday night. This will give me a chance to briefly see the children and talk to Angie about any future visits.

Ignoring all messages from Beth is helping me immensely. I have even told Will and Theo that they are not to put a Mrs Henderson through to me should she ring. By the end of my first week I am feeling more at home at the dealership and I am looking forward to giving the new car a bit of a run.

Theo and I leave Plymouth separately just after 3pm. I am glad that I am driving the first leg of my journey on my own. Frankly, I am already dreading sitting next to Theo later on and having to talk to him all the way back. Despite the golfing connection our boss-trainee relationship is still somewhat fragile.

I know that will encounter heavy traffic at this time of day but I am just relieved to be on the road. My trusty old car may not be as swish and smooth as the new Mercedes but I will miss it, no doubt about that. I have asked Jordan to tell Angie that I will be visiting in order to collect the rest of my personal effects tonight and I am hoping not to receive a frosty welcome. What I have not told my son is that I will be in the company of a rather arrogant young man.

The thought of visiting "home" is unbearable. Having returned the VW to its owners I now ride shotgun with Theo in my new car. I don't want to talk to him about my private life but he catches me fidgeting in my seat, my fingers leaving damp marks on the dashboard as we are turning into what used to be "our" road. A horrible feeling of nausea has got hold of me. When I tell Theo to stop outside "our" house he smiles and says: "It's fine, Rob, calm down. She won't kill you. Can't be easy going through a divorce. I'll wait in the car, if you like."

I want to say something nasty in reply but no words come out. All I do is nod, hoping that young Theo will understand.

Then I spot Jordan at the front door, waving his hands wildly when he recognises the writing on my car. "Dad, Dad!" he shouts so loudly that the neighbours can hear it. He is still limping slightly as he rushes up the drive to take a closer look at my new vehicle. "Nice car, Dad," he remarks admiringly as I get out. He completely ignores Theo in the driver's seat. I take my little boy into my arms. "Good to see you, mate," I say to him. We enter the house together. "Mum! Dad is here!" Jordan shouts up the stairs. I wait patiently until Angie comes down with Melanie. She says "hello" but nothing else. Like an uninvited visitor I wait to be asked to follow her into the lounge. She does not even ask me to take a seat.

Although I have not been given permission I drop into the sofa, like I always used to, but this time my hands are trembling like never before. Angie is in tears. Putting Melanie on the carpet first she sits down in the armchair opposite me, wiping her face with the back of her hand. "I still can't believe what you've done, Rob," she whimpers sadly. "At your leaving party - that was not the first time, was it? You had an affair with Beth Henderson before then, am I right?" she asks bravely. I feel awful, mortified. To hear the truth from Angie sounds worse somehow. In shame I bow my head but remain silent. "Why don't you admit it, Rob? I know it's a fact," she continues. Still unable to speak I pick Melanie up to take her into my arms.

"I don't expect you to apologise but you could at least show me some respect and stop lying, "Angie says. With that she gets up. "I'll make us a cup of tea," she suggests. While she is in the kitchen I play with my little daughter.

This is the final straw, no way back now. Our marriage is over once and for all. I am so glad that Jordan enters the lounge and takes Melanie off me. "I want you to have the kids next weekend," Angie says when she returns with the tea. "Sorry but I will be away with Justin," I respond immediately, feeling dreadful as I realise that my answer will not go down well. "It's your turn, Rob. You have to take some responsibility. You can't go off seeing friends or playing golf when it suits you anymore. Jordan is desperate to spend some time with you and Melly soon won't remember who you are," Angie argues.

Sighing I pull my phone out of my pocket. Any personal appointments are stored on it. At a quick glace I notice that I am required at work the weekend after next. "You'll have to change your plans, I am afraid," Angie insists. The thought of letting Justin down makes me feel uneasy but I am hoping that he will understand. "OK, my family comes first," I finally agree. "Thank you – and please tell your solicitor to hurry up," she urges me. I want to say something, explain something but I fail. Words cannot describe how sad I am. Putting my empty mug back on the coffee table I decide that I must leave right now. "I was hoping that we could have a good chat about all this," I say softly, getting up from the comfortable sofa. "There is nothing to discuss, Rob," Angie replies, sounding hostile. I don't agree but I don't argue and leave the house.

My new job is keeping me busy during the week. I cancel my planned outing with Justin and spend most evenings after work in the floodlit driving range, across the car park from my flat, practicing my swing. Hitting golf balls provides some relief from the daily stress. I can let my frustration out, both mentally and physically, but it is still a lonely existence.

The meeting with my new solicitor who happens to be a customer of my new firm is not very pleasant either. I still don't want to go ahead. It hurts me to get the proceedings started. The easiest task so far has been to persuade my current letting agent in Newquay to show my chosen estate agent around the cottage in Crantock. I cannot wait for the property to go on the market, no matter if I will have to share the proceeds of the sale with Angie or not. The thought of getting rid of the cottage seems strangely satisfying.

Beth has been on my mind constantly. At times I am tempted to ring her, tell her that I am definitely getting divorced and that I would like to see her. When I lie in bed I fantasise about living with her but each and every time I come to the conclusion that I am not ready for it.

Then the weekend starts, and Angie has given strict instructions for me to come and pick Jordan and Melanie up at 7pm on Friday evening and bring them back in the afternoon of Sunday.

It is my first "father's weekend" and my ex has prepared for it impeccably. There is a brand new holdall with all the children's clothes, nappies, some toys and most other equipment that they may require during the next couple of days and nights. Melanie's favourite teddy and Jordan's skin cream, even swimwear and beach towels – there is nothing that Angie has not thought about. She hands the kids over to me almost clinically. Melanie is crying, Jordan full of excitement.

"When we've been to your flat, Dad, can we go to your cottage again, please?" my son asks me as we finally drive out of Launceston. Now that he has had his plaster cast removed and his injured leg is feeling very much better he is itching to go to the beach. "I am trying to sell the cottage, Jordan. It's all nice and tidy there so I would prefer not to use it this weekend," I explain. "Sell? You can't sell that place, Dad! Your auntie wanted you to have it when she died. She wants you to look after all her belongings in the roof. You can't sell it!" Jordan argues quickly. His words make me smile. "When we went there the other day you didn't like the cottage – and besides, I cannot afford to keep another house going. I am paying for Mum, you and Melly to stay in your house and I have to pay rent for my new apartment," I reply sternly. "If you came back home with us you wouldn't have to pay for an apartment and then you could keep the cottage," Jordan suggests. I wonder why my son has changed his mind about the old property. Perhaps he has found something interesting in those photograph albums. I should ask to see them for myself sometime.

Melanie has gone to sleep in the back of my comfy new car. "I am sure Mum will have told you that I won't come back home. Mum and I won't be living together anymore," I say slowly. "Mum says that you have a girlfriend. Is that true?" Jordan wants to know. "No, it is not. I don't have a girlfriend. You can correct Mum on that," I answer, feeling a little annoyed. "Mum says the reason why you don't live with us anymore is because you have a girlfriend and you want to live with her," my son insists. "That's nonsense, Jordan," I say rather sharply.

This conversation is getting difficult. Pressing the accelerator harder I try to get the short journey to Saltash, where I now live, over and done with as soon as possible.

Once the "girlfriend" topic is out of the way Jordan proves to be of great help. He is looking after his little sister while I unload the car. According to Jordan my new apartment is "cool". I guess that is quite a positive statement although the sweat is pouring off me and I feel anything but "cool". For Melanie there is a good quality travel cot in the lounge but Jordan will have to spend the night on a worn out guest bed. "Can we go to the swimming pool in the morning?" my son asks. "Yes, of course. It's all part of the club here. I'll show you around after breakfast," I promise. Then we make a late evening trip to the supermarket in order to stock up for the weekend.

Having to feed Melanie as well as myself and Jordan is quite hard work. It seems that we are spending half the night in the kitchen. When I think about the fact that I should have been meeting up with Justin right now I feel rather sorry for myself. I love spending time with my children but the prospect of having to do this kind of thing every fortnight puts me off. Melanie does not settle too well in her cot tonight either. If she doesn't stop screaming soon I will be evicted from my accommodation before the weekend is over. Jordan is trying his utmost to assist but, to be honest, I think Melanie may be missing her mother.

Apart from anything else the "cool" apartment is fairly hot. Having finally got Melanie to sleep Jordan and I have difficulties settling ourselves. Our duvets are too thick so we feel uncomfortable and restless all night – not a great start to the "father's weekend". If only we could be a normal family, living at home under one roof, sharing the responsibilities!

I cope well with our breakfast the next morning. Warm sunshine is pouring in through the large lounge windows which allow a stunning vista right across the magnificent golf course towards the river Tamar. Jordan can't wait to get to the swimming pool. It will be his first swim since his injury and that is obviously exciting.

I am doing all the hard work though – washing up our dishes, packing our bags, making the beds, cleaning up under Melanie's highchair, changing nappies. No, I must not think about what could have been. Having a family is so much better than accompanying a friend to a car show or playing golf. OK, at the moment I feel that it is not, but I am sure I am wrong.

Before we go to the pool I show Jordan and Melanie around the vast Country Club premises. My son is impressed with the hotel and its outstanding sports facilities, the beautiful garden area and the adventure playground. It is simply paradise for Jordan and Melanie. "This place is great, Dad," my son exclaims happily. I have taken my eye off Melanie for just a second. As I turn around I can see her toddling off at an incredible speed. I never knew that my daughter was this fast before. Screeching excitedly she crosses the garden, waving her arms in the direction of the golf course. Jordan realises that she is heading for danger and half limping, half running, he follows her.

I am in fast pursuit of my children when my mobile rings. While Jordan has just caught up with his sister and pulls her off the fairway I answer the call. "Hi, it's Peggy from Wickers & Co," a friendly voice greets me. I walk on to lead my children towards the swimming pool when Peggy continues: "We've got someone interested in your cottage." I take a deep breath but I don't say anything. "In fact we have this morning received an offer," Peggy goes on. She is expecting me to comment but I am speechless. It's all a little too quick, too soon for me. "Mr Cunningham? It's only very slightly under the asking price," I hear Peggy say. I am not ready for this, not at all. "I, I'm not selling," I eventually stutter. "What do you mean?" Peggy's voice has suddenly taken on a strangely sharp tone. "I'm not selling under the asking price," I explain, pulling the children into the male changing room. A couple of elderly men shake their heads. "What is the little girl doing in here?" one of them asks, sounding quite affronted. It is impossible to talk business with my estate agent and explaining the circumstances of single parenthood at the same time. "I'll ring you back," I tell Peggy. In the meantime the two men have left the changing room and I rush to get Melanie into her swim suit and out of the embarrassing situation.

An offer on the cottage already! It's only been on the market for a couple of days. I cannot believe that the place is so popular. Surely the prospective purchaser must be someone from the village who has been waiting for my property to come up for sale. I enter the pool, completely out of my depth already. I can't concentrate on the offer, not now. Melanie struggles in my arms while Jordan is thoroughly enjoying his first swim for many weeks. Inevitably my eyes scan all the happy families around me in the water. There are Mums and Dads taking turns looking after their kids, brothers and sisters splashing about wildly, older couples swimming along quietly, the two chaps from the male changing room eagerly paddling from one end of the pool to the other and then there is me – lonely and feeling sorry for myself. "Don't look so miserable. I'll take Melly for a bit if you want to have a swim, Dad," Jordan eventually offers. I nod gratefully and hand Melanie over to him. Before she can protest I take off but I don't get very far as other bathers have the same idea. The pool is quite busy and hardly large enough to cope with heavy traffic. Turning around I can see Jordan distracting his sister by letting her ride on a teddy bear-shaped float. It appears that he has quickly learnt to deal with all the fatherly tasks in the house recently.

I am trying to relax but swimming is bound to bring back memories of those wonderful days in Crantock. I wore Brian's funky board shorts... It still has not sunk in properly that that day was the beginning of the end of my marriage. How could I let all this happen? As I am lying on my back in the water I think of Beth. It is no good. I must return to the children.

Jordan cannot get enough of the pool but I decide to take Melanie out of the water before she gets cold. Yet again I am facing the hostile world of the male changing room but no one is actually prepared to tell me off. After our swim I invite my kids for lunch at the hotel – madness, with a tired toddler and an excitable wannabe teenager but at least it saves cooking. I have totally forgotten to ring the estate agent back but somehow I don't feel in a rush to get the deal done today.

During the afternoon I take the children to Plymouth. Jordan claims that he needs some new football boots but his mother won't buy him any. With Melanie in the buggy life is much easier. She settles down nicely after lunch and is fast asleep while we are roaming the sports shops in the city. My son is in his element. "Thanks, Dad. I wonder what Mum will say when she sees these," he says, lifting the bag containing the most expensive pair of football boots up into the air. We end up buying a lot more than just boots. For a couple of hours the topic of Mum and Dad splitting up has been put on hold. Unfortunately, the sore subject returns on our way back to Saltash. "Mum doesn't want to admit it but she really misses you, Dad," Jordan suddenly says. Melanie is awake and chatting away next to him in the rear of the car. "How do you know?" I ask my son. Jordan goes to great lengths to explain why Angie finds it hard to live without me, and he tells me that his mother sometimes even cries. Then he asks: "And how about you, Dad? Do you miss Mum at all? Is there no way you two can make up again?" I don't want to answer these questions. They break my heart. Is this what I will get every second weekend from now on? "Listen, Jordan. I realise that you may think it is easy for me to simply come back and live with you three but it is no longer possible…," I start carefully as I turn into the drive of the Country Club. "Mum says it is all because you have a girlfriend," Jordan repeats firmly. "I don't have a girlfriend!" I correct him once again. Angrily I brake hard when parking the car. We all shoot forward in our seats but Jordan seems undeterred. It appears that Angie must have told him about this girlfriend business. "Mum says you love her more than Mum," Jordan insists. I am about to lose my temper. "Stop it, Jordan. There is no girlfriend or anything else – end of story," I shout furiously.

When I wake up the next morning I feel shattered. I have had another vivid dream about Beth. We were back in the cottage, making love. I could hear her breathe, feel her warm body next to mine. It was all so real that it takes me a couple of minutes until I can think clearly. Melanie is stirring in her travel cot. Very slowly I get up, shaking my head. I don't believe that I have ever dreamt like last night before. Picking my little daughter up, I sigh. What does this dream mean? Is it that I miss Beth? Is it that I miss sex? Are my feelings for her so much stronger than I am prepared to confess? I am still somewhat confused about my dream when Jordan gets up.

"Can we have another swim this morning, Dad?" my son asks. He is already off to the balcony to check if our trunks have dried over night. I nod submissively while feeding Melanie. "Great! The next time we come to stay with you I'll be ready to play you at tennis," Jordan says while taking the swimwear off the washing line. Dreading the thought of another weekend alone with my children I make no comment. I am just glad that they, or at least Jordan, are enjoying it.

Luckily this morning I have no problems taking my daughter with us into the male changing room. It seems that it is generally less crowded in the pool on Sundays. My mind remains troubled by last night's dream. Holding Melanie in my arms I wonder if I am going crazy. Other parents are smiling at me encouragingly but I am unable to shake this feeling of incompetence off. Jordan has met another boy at the far end of the pool. He looks of a similar age to my son. I watch the boys talking and then they are off practicing different strokes together. I am stuck in the shallow water with Melanie.

Later on we have lunch in my apartment and then we spend an hour at the children's play park in the sunshine until it is time to pack the kids' bags and return them to their mother. I am reasonably satisfied with the first "father's weekend" but I cannot say that I have truly enjoyed it. Both children seem strangely quiet on the way back to Launceston too.

Approaching my former home apprehensively I contemplate talking to Angie before returning to Saltash but then Jordan spots a red car outside the house. "Uncle Charlie and Auntie Barb are here!" he exclaims excitedly. Well, that puts an end to any plans of spending time with Angie then. While I get Melanie out of her car seat Jordan runs off to see my wife's best friends. Unhappily I carry my daughter and the bags down the drive. Angie appears on the door step, her face looking strained. "You are early," she remarks. "Yes, I am sorry. Is that a problem?" I reply apologetically. "No, it's just that I did not expect you yet," says Angie. Melanie is overjoyed to have her Mum back. "Phuh, you smell of chlorine," Angie points out when kissing our daughter's fine hair. "We've had a swim in the pool this morning," I explain. "OK, well, seems like you had a good weekend then," Angie simply says, taking the heavy bags off me. I wait to be asked in but my wife calls for Jordan. "Come here and say good-bye to Dad," she demands. Our son appears briefly and says: "Thanks, Dad." Then he disappears into the lounge where Charles and Barbara are. I find the situation awkward, somehow embarrassing, sad – very difficult to describe. The fact remains that I hate it, I really do. "My solicitor will be in touch regarding future arrangements," Angie tells me. And that's it. She turns around and closes the door behind her. For a couple of seconds I just stand there, staring at the front door. No good hoping for a miracle – it's time to leave.

Over the next few days I tell myself that I will have to get used to these weekends but at this moment in time I do not feel very confident about them. It is terribly quiet in my flat when I return from work each evening. After a busy day at the dealership I am often totally exhausted. The demands of my new job are much higher than I anticipated. When I drop into my rented sofa after an hour on the driving range I try to analyse why I find it so hard to get used to it. Why do I find it tough to cope with my role as Head of Department? I don't mind being the boss, taking responsibility, working in a competitive environment but somehow my staff and colleagues don't seem supportive – and I am not just talking about sleek young Theo who cannot wait to test my golfing abilities. It is the general feeling of unease and pressure, always having to fight my corner alone. I miss my family and friends. I miss the warmth and closeness of the small car dealership in Launceston. Most of all I miss home, coming back to a place of real comfort after work, kissing my wife and children, having dinner together, watching TV or having a discussion, going to bed – a regular family life.

So here I am in my luxury apartment, close to tears again. I still have not got back to the estate agent. Realising that it is by far too late in the day to speak to them I take a few minutes to consider my options and then I decide to ring. Patiently I am waiting for the answer phone to kick in. I leave a message confirming that I am definitely not going to accept any offers under the asking price.

As I am due to work on Saturday and Sunday the following weekend, I have been granted Thursday and Friday off instead. Early on Thursday morning Peggy rings me on my mobile. "I've got good news, Mr Cunningham. The purchaser is offering the full asking price!" she informs me. I am stunned, really did not expect that, not this soon. "That's...yes, gr-eat," I stammer helplessly. "It looks as if we will be moving very fast on this one, Mr Cunningham. The purchaser will send someone around to do a survey. I have told them about the roof and the poor overall condition of the cottage," Peggy says. Her words bring a strange kind of relief. What did my neighbour George say when he carried out the emergency repairs? *Nobody will buy a place like this unless the roof is fixed...* Perhaps this is all a storm in a tea cup and I don't have to worry about selling at all yet. I know how many time-wasters I deal with at the car showroom each and every day. Naturally I don't tell Peggy about my negative feelings but I promise her to get in touch with my solicitor to sort out the necessary legal matters. This means that my entire Thursday is taken up with exhausting phone calls, emails and resulting paperwork.

It transpires that the purchaser is not even local. Peggy tells me that he is from London, and he is buying the cottage without viewing it. Alarm bells ring loudly in my head but Peggy encourages me to be positive. She claims that this is not unusual for property sales in Cornwall but I am far from convinced. I have had my fair share of misfortune as far as the cottage is concerned, so how could I possibly think that this deal will be going through smoothly? Apart from anything else I still don't know how much of the proceeds from the sale will actually be mine. The whole affair is definitely moving too fast for me. It reminds me of dealing with the Hendersons – they don't give you time to catch your breath.

By early evening I realise that I will have to clear the attic, sooner rather than later. Recalling the amount of stuff in the roof space I calculate that it will take me a full day to sort the loft out. I look at my watch and spontaneously decide to pack an overnight bag and drive to Crantock. On my way I stop at the nearest DIY store. By now it is a few minutes to 8pm which means that the shop is about to close but I quickly manage to whizz around the aisles. All I need is a good-quality ladder that will fit into my new estate car. This will enable me to work in the attic on my own in the morning. The thought of routing through Aunt Delia's belongings is starting to excite me.

It is dark when I arrive in the village. In autumn you can tell immediately which houses are being lived in and which ones are holiday homes. Unless there are lights on inside or windows open it is quite obvious that the properties are empty. Even I have already learnt to interpret the badly timed security lights that most holiday home owners have in operation these days.

As I drive down the road towards the beach car parks I expect to find my cottage in complete darkness. To my absolute shock and surprise all the lights are on inside and the bathroom window is wide open. My heart is beating like a drum. Who on earth could be in the cottage? There are no cars parked outside. It is normally easy to park any vehicle in the space close to the granite retaining wall but my new car requires a little more careful manoeuvring. Feeling terribly nervous it takes me two attempts to squeeze my Mercedes in. Hesitantly I get out of the car and listen. There is loud music blaring out of the open window. No doubt about it, someone is in my cottage – and whoever it is does not seem afraid of drawing attention to this fact. Standing outside in the dark my mind works overtime. Has Beth had the key copied before returning it? Who, apart from me and my estate agent, would have a key? The contract with the letting agent has not been renewed...

It has started to rain and I am shivering. I can't just wait here. I must find out who is in my cottage. With that I pull my key out of the pocket of my old washed out jeans. Should I knock or ring the door bell? This is my property, why would I do that? My shaky fingers eventually manage to put the key into the lock. The Hendersons – it can only be Beth or her sons, Brian or...

Carefully I push the front door open. As I enter a man appears halfway down the narrow stairs. If I were a woman I would be knocked off my feet! The stranger is extremely tall and wearing nothing but a small white towel wrapped around his slim hips. He is well-tanned and even better built, with a proper six pack and massive broad shoulders. His slightly long blond hair looks wet – the perfect picture of a surfer dude. To say that I feel intimidated is putting it mildly.

I gulp, then shout against the music: "What are you doing here?" Waiting for a response I watch the stranger's long fingers re-fasten the towel. "I could ask you the same question. This is my property," he replies, not smiling. I recognise his accent immediately. He sounds Australian. Shaking from head to toe, partly due to the draught caused by the open bathroom window, I close the front door behind me. "Your property? I am the owner," I say bravely. My eyes follow the tiny pearls of water that are dripping from the stranger's hair onto the ancient oak floorboards of the staircase. Then I watch the beach boy run his left hand through his wet locks. "There must be a misunderstanding. I have inherited this cottage," he says calmly. With that he walks down the last few steps until he is on the same level as me. At barely 5ft 10in I feel like a miniature garden gnome compared to him. "So have I," I retort firmly. I guess the guy is not much older than me. His skin appears young and firm but his face looks more mature. "My mother left me this cottage," he explains. I don't know why but I stare at his bare feet and calf muscles. Naturally I don't believe him.

Having to look up to the stranger to talk to him makes me feel very inadequate but I say: "That wouldn't be my aunt Delia by any chance?" His striking blue eyes assess me for a second, before a big smile lightens up his handsome face. "Yes, Delia was my mother. You probably didn't know...anyway, nice to meet you. I am Fletcher," he says offering me his enormous hand. I shake it reluctantly, still shocked, still in awe of this fine figure of a man. "I'm Rob," I introduce myself.

"Looks like we have some talking to do," Fletcher says. I am quite surprised how confident he is. I nod silently. "Let me turn the radio off and get dressed. Have you come to stay the night?" he asks. Somehow I have not expected this question and it throws me. "Yes, yeah, well, I don't know now..," I stutter. "Right, bring your luggage in, if you have any. The place is well equipped, and you can have the spare room," Fletcher says. That guy has got a nerve – and the arrogance with it! It annoys me that he treats me like a visitor in my own home. "Listen, I am the legal owner of this property. You can't tell me what to do," I reply furiously. Fletcher chooses to ignore my statement. "I haven't got much in the house. I would suggest we nip over to the pub and discuss the situation there," he says. I have noticed that he is not just very aloof but also well spoken. My little outburst has not bothered him in the slightest. "You obviously know the village. How long have you been here?" I ask, still not sure what to make of him. "I arrived yesterday and had a quick look around. Do you think we are going to make it before closing time?" He is not waiting for me to answer. When I turn around he is already upstairs getting dressed.

Shaking my head in disbelief I leave the cottage to bring my bag in from the car. My new ladder stays in the boot. I am determined to stand my ground. No way is this Fletcher who claims to be my cousin going to boss me around. When I return indoors he is fully dressed, trying to dry his hair with another towel. It is one of mine, belonging to the cottage. "I'm ready, let's go," Fletcher says, pulling on a light cardigan. His clothes look of good quality. I secretly wonder what he does for a living. Walking along the road I have a job to keep with him.

Minutes later we are in the pub, among the locals who made me feel so uncomfortable the last time I came here. Nobody would ever feel vulnerable or awkward in Fletcher's company though. The way he looks he just doesn't go unnoticed. You wouldn't mess with a man like him, I am quite sure about that. Although I am still unsure of his identity I am prepared to buy my newly found cousin a beer but he insists on paying. Then we retreat into a cosy corner and start talking – or to be more precise – Fletcher starts talking. The guy is incredible. "I am not just here to take possession of the cottage," he explains. "It has taken me a long time to make this trip. I had many months of research to do before I felt ready to book my flights. It appears that I was conceived in that cottage up the road. Of course, my mother was not married at the time, and so far I have no idea who my biological father is and what actually happened. Anyhow, my mother was pregnant with me and felt that she had to leave the UK. She told me that herself, "Fletcher says, pausing and sipping his lager. He takes a deep breath before continuing: "She went to Australia to start a new life – and, of course, to give birth to me. However, there was a problem. I was a large baby and there were complications," again Fletcher pauses, "I don't want to bore you with the details but to cut her medical history short – she was no longer able to have children after I was born," Fletcher explains. "She told me that the birth and its aftermaths were very traumatic and she could not face looking after me. So she gave me up for adoption. I was very lucky. The couple who adopted me were absolutely wonderful. They loved me so much. I had a stable home and received a great education. They even helped me research my roots when I turned 18. I found my mother, Delia, when I was in my early twenties. We kept in touch but it was never a very close relationship. She refused any information about my biological father. Besides I felt that I could not put her through all the painful memories."

As Fletcher pauses yet again I realise how intently I have been listening. I have not even drunk half of my pint and the landlady is urging us to drink up. "I'll buy us a couple of bottles to take home," Fletcher suggests. With that he gets up to speak to the landlady.

I cannot believe how this evening has turned out. Fletcher's story has made me forget everything I have come to Crantock for. I don't know if I like him but when I hear him talk I detect kindness, something in his foreign voice that makes him trustworthy. Now he waves at me. "Come on, Rob. Time to turn in!" he shouts. Like an obedient child I follow him, back up the road to our cottage. Fletcher is carrying the bottles. As it is still raining we walk fast. Arriving outside the front door we both pull our keys out at the same time. We chuckle and Fletcher lets me use my key. Both of us proceed straight to the kitchen. This is starting to become ridiculous. Again we chuckle. Then Fletcher asks me if I require a glass for my beer. "I'm happy to drink from the bottle," I reply. "Great!" Fletcher says and with that he uses the sole of his fine leather shoes to open the bottles. *Aussie trick*, I think but I don't say anything.

We sit down in the lounge where it is not very warm. The rain has become much heavier too and it is now drumming violently against the single-glazed windows. "Just made it in time by the look of it," comments Fletcher. He does not seem to feel the cold. My cousin has his long legs crossed, completely filling out the old armchair he is sitting in. "Where did I get to?" he asks me. "Your mother, my aunt, not telling you about your father," I remind him. "Yeah, right, that's why I am here. I want to know who he is or was and if there are any relatives," he says. He looks suddenly very serious, not quite as snooty and over-confident as a few minutes ago. I don't know why but I am starting to warm to him. "OK, I understand that but who told you that you have inherited this place?" I ask. "I've got a letter. It was with the key," Fletcher responds. He gets up to fetch the document. I use the time to empty my bottle. The cold beer makes me feel even colder than I am already.

Fletcher returns with the letter. "This cottage meant a lot to my mother – here, have a read," he says, passing me a hand-written A4-sized page.

Melbourne, 20th January 2016

Dear Fletch, my Son,

This will find you when I have passed away. I hope you won't be too upset. My illness was getting me down. It was terrible, perhaps the punishment for what I have done when I was younger, punishment for giving you up – you, my only child, my son.

Margaret and Jeff have brought you up well. I am eternally grateful for that. Please forgive me for refusing to meet them but you told me so much about them that I feel I know them quite well.

My marriage to Todd was a disaster, like most things in my life, but that is over now. He does not know about you – I never told him. It was better that way.

It takes me some considerable effort to write clearly and coherently. So I have to keep it brief.

You have a right to know about my past. Todd knows that I have a brother in the UK. We fell out years ago. Neither Todd nor my brother knows that I own the property where you were conceived - a small cottage in a beautiful village in Cornwall. The village is called Crantock and it is near Newquay. I have not been back there for many years but you will find the cottage is called "Primrose". It never had a house number.

I know it is a long way for you to go but enclosed is the key. It should still fit. I have been in contact with my agent in Newquay not so long ago. The property is being let as holiday accommodation so it's best to visit when the English summer holidays are over.

I want you to have the cottage. It is all I can give you. That little cottage still means so much to me. It was the only place where I have been truly happy – if only for a season.

Good-bye, take care, look after yourself and your lovely family. I am proud of you.

Love
Your Mum xxxx

On the reverse of the letter Delia has printed the name of the letting agent, complete with address and phone number.

I am moved, feeling quite sombre when handing the letter back to Fletcher. "I had no idea," I say softly. Fletcher folds the letter up neatly. Then he looks at me. "And how about you? How did you come to inherit this?" he wants to know. I sigh. "I had a letter from a legal firm in London advising me that this cottage was bequeathed to me," I reply. Fletcher gets up and paces up and down the small lounge - very irritating! He is so incredibly patronising. Despite it all, deep down I still wish I could kick him out. "So you've got the deeds, all the necessary papers," he concludes. I nod silently. "In that case I will have to contest my mother's will," Fletcher says firmly. I can feel the heat rising into my cheeks, my heart rate increasing by the second. "I am in the process of selling," I tell him. Fletcher shakes his head. "Selling what is not even yours? Hang on a minute, Rob," he shouts. This is the first time since I have met him that he is losing his impressive composure. "I've come here tonight to clear the attic out in the morning. You will find the mess up there of interest - it's all your mother's stuff," I inform him.

He frowns. His blond locks have dried out. In the dim light of the lounge he looks like a gigantic angel.

"I'll help you empty the loft out but I would very much appreciate it if you could put the sale on hold for a while - first thing in the morning," he suddenly pleads. Having read his mother's emotional letter I don't have the heart to refuse. "OK," I agree without any further thought. Fletcher starts pacing up and down again. I have not expected it but he turns to me, puts his large hand on my shoulder and says: "Thank you."

It is well after midnight when we go to bed. Fletcher is in the double room and I am in the single, the room with the damp ceiling. It is not the most pleasant experience. Everything, and in particular the bedding, has taken on that horrible mouldy odour. I lie here, staring at the stained walls where the ingress of water has left marks and wonder what is happening to me. I have a restless night and feel absolutely shattered in the morning.

At least the weather has improved dramatically. As the dawn chorus has started I take a quick look out of the window and check the time on my mobile phone. It is 6am. I sit up in my smelly single bed and listen. The radio is on - sounds like my cousin is up already. Shaking my head I climb out of bed and make my way to the bathroom. "Good morning, fancy a run?" Fletcher greets me. He is fully dressed in running gear, all the latest and the best, of course. His blond hair is tied back neatly. Standing there in just my old underpants makes me feel like a lower class citizen. I yawn. "Well, I wouldn't mind but I didn't bring any sportswear...," I stutter. Fletcher smiles. I am sure he must think that I am making excuses. "No problem. I'll kit you out. You'll be fine with my shorts and if the top is a bit big and baggy it doesn't really matter. The trainers you wore last night will be OK, too," he says. Well, that's that then. There is no way out. Within ten minutes I wear yet another man's shorts, a bright yellow t-shirt and my old trusted trainers. Then we are off.

It is amazingly beautiful outside. The air is so still, apart from the bird song. On the horizon the sun is about to rise and everything smells fresh and salty, cool and invigorating. Only the tarmac of the road leading to the beach car parks reminds us of the heavy rain last night. Every step we take creates a squidgy sound under our trainers, and now and again we have to circumnavigate large puddles. We jog along easily until we reach the lower car park. "The tide should be out, so we are OK to run along the beach," Fletcher suggests. We are the only fitness fanatics out this early in the morning. As we run up the steep dune I begin to struggle whereas Fletcher's long legs carry him up the sandy hill without any problems. "What do you do for a living?" I ask my cousin as we finally reach the water's edge. The firm damp sand underfoot makes it easier to run. "I'm a surgeon – in orthopaedics. I specialise in knee surgery," he replies without slowing down. "I, I see," I stutter, fighting against the strong wind to keep up with him. We are heading towards West Pentire. In the distance we can see the great dark cliffs where Beth showed me that special cave, the one with the carvings. "And you?" Fletcher wants to know. "Car Sales, Mercedes," I reply huffing and puffing. Fletcher's phenomenal speed takes my breath away. I hope that my cousin still remembers his basic medical training should I collapse from exhaustion. Perhaps I should show him that cave – at least it would make us stop for a while. I am starting to lag behind, panting.

Luckily nature lends me a helping hand. We have reached the end of the long beach where the tide has left a rather wide and deep gully. I guess that Fletcher is considering a jump but suddenly he stops right in front of it. "Sounds like I am working you a little too hard, Rob," he says. His sparkling blue eyes are assessing my heaving chest critically. "Yes," I reply, still puffing, "yes, you are a lot fitter than me," I admit, trying to catch my breath. Fletcher smiles kindly. "I am quite impressed that you kept going for this long, to be honest," he says. He has not even broken sweat yet. I am too tired to reply. "Let's turn back, jogging slowly, so we won't cool down too much," Fletcher proposes. I nod gratefully. At the same time I wonder if my cousin has taken in the stunning views across the vast ocean, the lovely blue sky and magnificent scenery. "How old are you?" he asks me on the way home. "Just turned 40 and you?" "I'll be 44 in December," he replies. I am starting to fade again and decide to walk for a bit instead of jogging. "Married?" Fletcher, who annoyingly is still jogging along with ease, asks. "In the process of getting divorced," I reply, feeling awful as usual. "Ah, is that why you want to sell the cottage?" Fletcher asks. I don't know why but he gives up his irritatingly slow jog and walks next to me now. I nod sadly, still breathing heavily. "What happened?" he wants to know. I am contemplating telling him to mind his own business but I say: "Long story but basically I have been a fool." Fletcher resists a comment. "Children?" he asks as we climb up the steep dune again. We pass a couple of dog walkers before I respond: "Boy and girl – eight and almost two." I notice that Fletcher slows down even more. We are virtually crawling across the lower beach car park. "My wife is called Sarah and we have a daughter, " he tells me. I can't explain it but something in his voice sounds weak. As we reach the road I am beginning to feel better, less exhausted. Fletcher has suddenly gone quiet.

"If you don't mind I will use the shower first. I'd like to catch the estate agency as soon as it opens," I say as we reach the cottage. Fletcher agrees that I should ring them at the earliest opportunity. He even offers to cook us breakfast.

I go to the lounge to make my phone calls. Mobile phone reception in the old granite cottage tends to be poor but fortunately I know a spot by the window where a conversation is normally successful. Both the estate agent and my solicitor warn me that the sale may well fall through if I delay proceedings. "So be it," I tell Peggy from Wickers & Co angrily. My gut instinct tells me that this "too good to be true" sale is not actually going to happen anyway.

A couple of minutes later I return to the kitchen. Fletcher has been frying bacon. It smells delicious, and I am beginning to feel very hungry. "All done," I say. I can't help observing my cousin's work at the hob. If he hadn't told me differently I would have guessed he is a professional chef. "Thank you, Rob. I appreciate that. You know," he says while filling our plates, "this place reminds of my student days!" As I watch him I wonder why I trust him so much. So far I have not had any proof that this man is who he pretends to be. How can I be sure that the letter he has shown me is genuine? I have not seen Fletcher's passport or any other document that will prove his identity. He could well be a chef rather than a surgeon.

"Enjoy," he says as we start our breakfast. "How long will you be staying in Cornwall?" I ask him. "Two weeks, initially. Should it be necessary I may be able to return for another fortnight in December," he replies. Again, I detect a trace of sadness in his voice. "I won't send you away now but unless you can prove that you have a legal right to this cottage I will eventually go ahead with a sale," I threaten. "Yes, I understand," Fletcher concedes. Our conversation is slow, almost tense, until it is time for me to fetch my new ladder.

Needless to say, it is I who has to creep into the dusty roof space. On my hands and knees I am pushing ancient suitcases and heavy boxes around until they are close enough to the trap door for Fletcher to lift them down. I have to admit that my cousin is a great help. His physical fitness and ability to concentrate for long periods of time make him a most efficient worker. By lunch time most of my Aunt

Delia's belongings are in the bedrooms. Fletcher has sorted everything into neat piles and taken photographs on his mobile phone. I catch him looking through the images. "Nothing much to help you find your roots, I'm afraid," I say as I remove my aunt's rusty putter from the old leather golf bag. "Do you play golf?" I ask then. "Used to. Don't have the time these days," he answers. "I played professionally until I realised I wasn't good enough to earn a decent living," I tell him. Dreamily I go through the useless set of clubs. "Wow! I hope you still play though – for fun, I mean," Fletcher replies. "Yes, now and again," I say vaguely. With that I shoulder the dust-covered bag in readiness to take it to my car. "This will have to go to the rubbish dump," I decide."Make sure you have checked all the pockets before you throw anything away," Fletcher instructs me. His words remind me that I still have that ring that Beth gave me in my golf bag. "You are right – will do," I promise.

My nice new estate car is soon full up with bags and boxes. Fletcher and I have decided to take some of the old clothes and bric-a-brac to the charity shop. "My son has a few photograph albums that we rescued from up here when the roof was leaking. I expect you would like to see them, "I say as I load the car. "Yes, that would be great. After lunch I will go through all the books and the more valuable items," Fletcher agrees. Although we only met yesterday we are starting to become good friends. Having worked so hard together this morning I invite my cousin out for a bite to eat. We freshen up and I drive him over to the Bowl Inn, a large pub and restaurant at West Pentire, less than ten minutes drive away from the cottage.

"This really is an amazing location," Fletcher comments as we reach the pub's car park. I have to confess that the view is fantastic on a sunny day like today. We look out to Crantock Bay where the tide is rolling in, wild waves crashing against the black rocks. Noisy seagulls are circling high above the lively waters. In the distance the vast golden beach looks deserted, clean and beautiful. It is too cold for us to sit outside but we manage to get a table by the window where we can enjoy the panoramic view. I catch Fletcher staring out to sea, looking sad again. "If you have to come over to England again you should bring your family," I say. "That's not so easy," Fletcher replies. His big hands search his pockets for his mobile phone. Within seconds he has the device ready to show me a picture of his daughter. Our meal has just been served but I have lost my appetite. The shock must be written all over my face. What I see on the small screen is a thin, pale teenage girl connected to what I assume is a dialysis machine. I don't know what to say. It has hit me like a knife.

"This is Caitlin. She's 14 and needs a new kidney. Unfortunately I am not a suitable donor nor is Sarah and the waiting list is too long. Time is running out – that's why I am looking for any relatives who may be prepared to become donors," Fletcher explains. He picks up his cutlery and begins to tuck into his lunch. I watch him, unable to follow suit. "How close a relative are you looking for? Could I be tested?" I ask immediately. Fletcher's blue eyes assess me almost lovingly. "Anyone can be tested as long as they are fit and healthy. They don't have to be related," my cousin responds. "I am, well, I think so anyway," I confirm eagerly. "It's quite a process, Rob. It has huge implications – for you and for the recipient. Please don't let your meal go cold. I am sorry, this was perhaps not an appropriate time to tell you," Fletcher apologises. He has nearly finished his lunch and I have not even started yet. The picture of my cousin's sick daughter will not leave my head. Suddenly I feel like a man on a mission. I want to know more. I want to help.

On the way back to the cottage I encourage Fletcher to tell me more about Caitlin and her outlook for the future. I am determined to find out all about kidney donation and offer to make an appointment with my GP next week. This topic has completely taken over. "Go easy, please, Rob. Becoming a living donor is a big decision. Don't build your hopes up. There is no guarantee that you can help but I appreciate your offer, of course," Fletcher says.

We are back in the cottage now. I brush out the empty loft and my cousin is sorting through heaps of dusty books. We have the radio on but I cannot think of anything else than the kidney matter.

Fletcher has found a couple of loose photographs that have been used as book marks. "Do you recognise anyone in these?" he asks once I have closed the trap door to shut the remaining dust in. "Yes, this one – I think this could well be my Dad!" I exclaim. My finger points at a small child in shorts, holding an older girl's hand. "Delia and my father were born nine years apart. They never got on once they were adults. That's what Dad said anyway," I say. "If I am not mistaken your father must be 68 now," Fletcher calculates. "Would have been. He died three years ago aged 65 – heart attack, very sudden," I clarify. I realise immediately that this information must come as a huge disappointment to Fletcher as, theoretically, my father would have been another relative suitable for testing. "I'm sorry," my cousin says. I don't know if those words are meant for me or for himself.

We stop to have a break from sorting personal effects. I go downstairs to make us a cup of tea. It is about time that I tell Fletcher that I am not going to stay another night. I have to work in the morning and on Sunday. Although I only live an hour away I would prefer to go back to Saltash tonight rather than early in the morning. Fletcher is on his ipad when I return with the drinks. I pass him a mug and inform him that I will be leaving around 6pm. "That's fine, Rob. I am quite capable of looking after myself. I've got plenty of work to do. I'll email you with the medical information and the details you require for your doctor – a warning, you may find it unsuitable for bedtime reading." He chuckles. I nod confidently but something inside me has changed. I feel both excited and also scared, very scared.

After communicating with Fletcher by email over the weekend I cannot wait to get in touch with my GP surgery in Launceston on Monday morning. When asked to confirm my address over the telephone I truthfully state my new details. "If you have moved to Saltash you will have to register there, sir," the female receptionist insists. I am furious, shouting at the polite young woman at the other end of the line, explaining that I only want to have a blood test, that I am trying to save a life but to no avail. They categorically refuse an appointment.

I make the call from my office, hoping that no one has overheard my outburst. Too late – having put the phone down my fist hits the desk. As I look up Theo's slender frame appears at the door. "'you alright, Rob?" he asks. I sigh. "I don't suppose you know of any doctor's surgeries in Saltash, Theo?" True to his always perfect and "know-all" nature Theo supplies the number of a health centre in my new home town. He even offers to enquire if they accept any new patients. "Thank you, Theo but I'd rather deal with that myself," I refuse. The trainee shrugs his shoulders and leaves my office.

Ten minutes later I have my appointment for the next morning. No one would believe how keen I am to get this initial blood test done. It feels as if my life has suddenly taken on a new direction. I find it hard to concentrate on my work. Fletcher has asked me to take it easy, one step at a time, but my mind is racing ahead. What if I am a potential match? What if I am not? I spend my lunch break looking at the internet, researching the topic of kidney donation in the UK and Australia.

Then I remember that I have promised Fletcher the photograph albums that Jordan took home. I send my son a text asking him if I could pick them up next weekend or even before. Unless we find a clue among those well-kept albums, I fear, it will be difficult for Fletcher to trace his father. So far I have avoided involving my mother. She has not been well recently and my marriage break-up has affected her badly. As it is quiet in the office this afternoon I decide to ring her. After we have talked about the weather, her health and my wellbeing I get to the point. "I'd like to come and talk to you about Aunt Delia," I start. I can hear my mother sighing. "I don't know much about her, Rob. I've never met her. Your Dad refused to talk to her. Strangely enough Jordan gave me some of Delia's photograph albums the other day. He told me that Angela did not want them in her house," my mother says then. "And? Did you have a look at them?" I ask. "Yes, I did. There were a couple of your Dad as a boy but I did not recognise the people in the later pictures. All I learnt is that Delia was quite a sportswoman, always winning trophies. Now I know where you get your golfing talent from, son!" I ignore her remark but I am determined to get my hands on the albums as soon as possible.

It is time for me to get back to my office work. Having arranged to see my mother at the end of the week I pick up the paperwork on my desk. I wish I did not have to deal with that right now. My head is buzzing and my mind still elsewhere. Jordan's text in reply to mine is not very satisfying either. "*Albums are at Gran's. Miss you, Dad x*", are his words. I miss him and Melanie too but I do not respond. The sales figures on the computer screen in front of me are starting to dance wildly, like little green ants, moving rapidly up and down. I have to get up from my office chair to get away from them. Maybe a thorough health check won't do me any harm.

Apart from my blood test and making an appointment with my new GP for the following week nothing remarkable happens over the next few days. The constant text messages and calls from Beth have suddenly stopped which is a great relief. It has been tough to leave them all unanswered but I am proud of the fact that I have managed to resist.

On Friday afternoon I hand my office work over to Will and Theo. They are both prepared to stay on late to see customers, man the telephone and complete any documentation that I have not been able to attend to. I can see both queuing up for my job soon if I don't get a better grip on my personal circumstances.

As usual I have to fight my way through heavy Friday rush hour traffic to get out of Plymouth but once I am on the road towards Launceston I feel strangely free. I have not seen my mother for some weeks and I am looking forward to her home cooking. Angie has been in touch to ask if I would take the children over the weekend. She also had another go at me for slowing the divorce proceeding down again. I try hard to stay calm, telling her that my solicitor now deals with all my affairs and that it is not my fault but inevitably our conversation ends up in an unpleasant shouting match. No doubt Jordan will be reporting what is really going on in my former home.

After dinner I tell my mother about my cousin. My description of his good looks makes my mother get up from the table. She returns with one of the albums and turns the pages over, right to the very end. "I was wondering who this is," she says. With that she takes my empty dinner plate away and replaces it with the album. "Any resemblance?" she asks. I am staring at a professionally taken photograph of a middle-aged man in a well-cut suit. The man in the picture is tall and blond, not quite as well-built as Fletcher and his hair is less curly and much shorter but there is just a chance. His features are handsome, not dissimilar to Fletcher's. "Absolutely no clue in here who this could be?" I ask. With that I push the album further up the table. My mother shakes her head. "No. I don't think he is in any other photographs and there is no caption," she replies. An entire page has been dedicated to the image of this well-dressed man. The photograph appears to be stuck down firmly. "I will get Fletcher to remove the photo to see if it says anything on the back," I say to my mother. I am tempted to tell her about Caitlin but then I decide that it is too early. What I do though is send Fletcher a message telling him that I may have some interesting news for him and that I will be coming to stay over the weekend, including my two children.

   "Great. Looking forward to seeing you all," he replies instantaneously. Before settling down on my mother's pull-out sofa bed for the night I take another good look at the person in the photograph album. This could well be the man Fletcher is looking for. Exciting times!

When Jordan, Melanie and I arrive in Crantock the next morning Fletcher is out. Jordan is disappointed. "I want to see my new uncle," he moans. "Maybe he is out running," I say while carrying our luggage into the cottage. Jordan shakes his head. "No, his running shoes are here," he deducts, lifting a sandy pair of trainers off the bottom step of the narrow staircase. Melanie has toddled off to the kitchen. I have taken my eyes off her for two seconds and her little hands have grabbed the thin cable of Fletcher's ipad that he must have left on the worktop. Smiling she carries the slim device by its charging lead from the kitchen to the lounge. Fortunately, Jordan catches up with her. "No, Melly, that's not ours," he tells her quickly. Carefully my son removes the shiny ipad from her curious fingers. "Wow, that's a super good one," Jordan comments as he cleans up the screen with the front of his t-shirt."Is Uncle Fletcher very rich?" he wants to know. "I expect so, Jordan. He has a good job," I reply. We just manage to return the ipad to the kitchen before Fletcher comes back.

He is laden with shopping bags. Both Jordan and Melanie stare at him in the same way I did when I first met him. The only difference is that today Fletcher is fully dressed and his face is almost entirely hidden behind the untamed golden locks. It falls to me to introduce everyone. Melanie is not quite sure about Uncle Fletcher but I can sense that Jordan would immediately describe him as "cool". "Well, I thought I'd better get some supplies in for the four of us," Fletcher explains. "I could have gone shopping by car," I reply awkwardly. Jordan offers to unpack the bags. While he is alone in the kitchen I take Melanie into my arms and signal to Fletcher. I point at the pile of photograph albums that I have deposited on the old coffee table. "Please, take a look," I encourage my cousin. I watch him intently as he browses through every one. "My mother does not recognise anyone apart from my Dad as a child," I remark, eagerly waiting for Fletcher to discover the man in the suit. "I've made enquiries in the village. There are a couple of residents around who remember my mother buying Primrose Cottage," Fletcher starts, and he adds: "And I am going to see a lawyer about the will next week."

All of a sudden I feel uneasy again. So, contesting Delia's will is not an idle threat. Is there a chance that Fletcher will be taking the cottage away from me? I observe that he is less intrigued by the blond man's photograph than Mum and I. "I will have to remove all the photos and see if there are any dates printed on the backs," he says slowly. Then he turns to me and asks: "When will you get the results of your blood test?" "Next week – I am going to discuss them with my new doctor," I answer truthfully. "I've spoken to Sarah last night. Caitlin is deteriorating. I shouldn't have made this trip," Fletcher says sadly. Again, he walks nervously up and down, just like he did in the night I met him. "Maybe we can chase the results up sooner, I, I mean, I don't know...," I stutter. My heart goes out to Fletcher. Holding my healthy little daughter in my arms I feel blessed. It must be unbearable for my cousin to watch.

Unsure how to cheer Fletcher up I suggest that we should go out for a walk. Jordan has joined us in the lounge now, and he points out that it will be impossible to take Melanie to the beach in her push-chair. "The young lady can ride on my shoulders. It's not too far to go," Fletcher offers. I have my doubts that my daughter will enjoy sitting up at the great height of 6ft 5in but I am willing to give it a go. Jordan wonders if there is a ball in the cottage. "No ball games, son. Your leg has only just healed," I say strictly. Then I explain to Fletcher that Jordan has had an accident playing football not so long ago. Disappointedly Jordan looks up to my cousin. "We'll pop into the post office and shop and see if they have something light, something that your sister can play with as well," he proposes. It is hard to argue with someone who knows all about broken bones so I dare not disagree.

It is a mild autumn day, a little dull but not unpleasant. Jordan and Fletcher are off to the post office and shop while I get Melanie changed. I hope that spending time with us will take my cousin's mind off his problems. Once Jordan and Fletcher have returned with an end-of-season bargain we get Melanie up onto the surgeon's shoulders. To my absolute surprise my daughter loves it. She is smiling and chattering away, her hands digging happily into Fletcher's blond curls. "If I end up bald I'll hold you responsible," my cousin says jokingly. We all laugh and then we walk down the road towards the beach.

Jordan can't wait to kick the ball around. He has already found out that "cool" Uncle Fletcher is prepared to get stuck into anything physical. Watching the tall man charge through the sand like an oversized child makes me smile. My son is also in his element. I have not seen him having so much fun for a long time. The light-weight ball gets accidentally kicked into the sea a couple of times and is swiftly carried away by the powerful waves. As I am looking after a frustrated Melanie who would like to join in the fun but who is clearly by far too young, I don't have to run after the ball. Both Fletcher and Jordan end up in the water, getting soaked. The sea is terribly cold this time of year making both man and boy shiver. "I am glad that the ocean is warmer where I live," Fletcher tells Jordan. "Cool. Do you go swimming every day?" my son wants to know. "No, Jordan, I don't have time. Some people do though," he replies. I listen in trepidation, hoping that Jordan will not ask any questions about Caitlin. I have told him in the car on the way here that Fletcher's daughter is not well. Melanie has started digging up soft sand and has put some of it into her eyes in the process. She is crying now. "Time to have lunch, folks," I suggest as my stomach is rumbling. We are all too cold and too sandy to go to the pub so we decide to have a light meal back in the cottage.

After lunch Fletcher carefully dissects the photographs albums. Melanie has an afternoon nap in her travel cot while Jordan and I watch the surgeon's skilled fingers remove each picture. Some of the photographs carry a date on the back, others not but there is nothing that would point Fletcher to his biological father. When my cousin gets to the photograph of the well-dressed man he has to use a kitchen knife to separate it from its page. "Bingo!" I call out as Fletcher finally removes the photo. There is a newspaper cutting stuck to the back of the picture. The paper has turned rather yellow over the years but we recognise the man in the once black and white, head and shoulders shot. I read the headline out aloud. It is printed in fat typeface: Disgraced Gynaecologist struck off...

Jordan and I watch Fletcher's blue eyes scan the article. In contrast to me he is not reading anything out aloud but when it comes to the name of the specialist concerned he repeats to us: "Colin Alfred Fletcher...Mr Fletcher..." Shaking his head Fletcher passes me the cutting. I suddenly wish I didn't have to read it but I feel that I have to. "What does it say, Dad?" Jordan asks eagerly. I have only read about four lines when I respond: "That this man was not very nice, not nice at all." While I finish reading the article Fletcher gets up and returns with his ipad. He quickly types the name Colin Alfred Fletcher into the device. The search results seem to be pouring in fast. It does not take long until my cousin hands me his slim computer. There are a couple of different photographs. Taken from another angle the images show a striking resemblance to Fletcher. The article below them reads: "....*Fletcher who was serving a lengthy prison sentence for botching hundreds of operations died in prison aged 63. It was reported that the disgraced surgeon suffered from a brain tumour and refused treatment...*"

There is a moment of silence. I can see my son frowning. He does not understand what is going on. My cousin and I look at each other, grim expressions on our faces. Then Fletcher picks up the original photograph from the table once more. He takes another close look at it and says: "I need a beer – will you join me?" I nod affirmatively and send Jordan to the kitchen to fetch the drinks. "I am so sorry, Fletch. You have not deserved all this bad news," I say helplessly. The large man looks small all of a sudden. I can't be sure but it appears that my cousin is fighting tears. He is trying so hard to be brave and stay in control of his emotions. "My Mum, my adopted Mum I mean, always told me that I could well be named after an Englishman by the surname of Fletcher. I dismissed that idea as too obvious and I failed to ask Delia about it before she died," he mumbles under his breath. "You can tell your Mum that she was right now," I say slowly. Fletcher shakes his head. "I'm afraid not, Rob. Both my adopted parents were killed by an avalanche in New Zealand the year that Sarah and I got married. It was a horrendous tragedy. Without Sarah I would never have got over it." I am glad that Jordan returns with the beers. My cousin could really do with something stronger but there are no spirits in the cottage. "Caitlin's illness almost drove us apart but I cannot forget what Sarah did for me when we got the news of the avalanche. My adopted parents were the only fatalities. All other members of the walking group survived. Mum and Dad were at the front, way ahead of the rest of the group. They did not stand a chance..."

As I put the cold glass of the beer bottle to my lips I realise that my cousin has in fact lost two sets of parents, an unusual and most tragic case. I have no words, don't know how to deal with this terribly sad situation, but I am just glad that Fletcher was not alone in the cottage when he found out about his father. "Would you like us to leave, Fletch? Perhaps you need a little time to digest all this," I offer. My young son is also looking very concerned now. "Are you alright, Uncle Fletch?" he asks assessing the tall man slumped into the old armchair opposite us. I quickly put my arm around Jordan. "Come on, son. We'll go back to Saltash when Melly wakes up. Fletcher needs some space," I say and get up.

"Please, don't go. I'd like you to stay. I am grateful for your company," Fletcher begs instantly. I nod slowly. Both the newspaper cutting and the photograph are still lying on the coffee table in front of us. I pick both items up and put them back into the album. Then I encourage Jordan to leave the lounge with me. "What did that man do, Dad?" Jordan enquires. "He was a very bad doctor and had to go to prison – but it is a long time ago and he is dead now, "I explain in simple terms once I have closed the door behind us. Jordan is not satisfied with my answer. "So why is Uncle Fletch so upset?" he wants to know. In moments like this I find it difficult being a parent. My son expects a response. "Uncle Fletcher thinks he is related to this man. He thinks he was named after him," I start awkwardly. Before I can continue Melanie stirs in her cot. "I'd like to give Fletcher a little time on his own, Jordan. Let's take Melly out in her pushchair for half an hour," I suggest quickly. I can see that my son is not enamoured by the idea but he does not argue.

It is not until we all go to the pub for our dinner in the early evening that Fletcher and I get the opportunity to discuss our findings. Fletcher has shown Jordan a computer game on his ipad so my son is occupied, and I am entertaining the highchair-bound Melanie with the usual beer mat tricks while we are talking. "I have done some more research on the internet while you were out," Fletcher starts, "I can only assume that my mother had an affair with Colin Fletcher. When she found out that she was pregnant and he was being investigated she fled the country – would make sense, don't you think?" my cousin says. I nod silently. "Maybe that's what I should have done," I whisper carelessly. "Running away is never the answer. My mother suffered the consequences for the rest of her life. We all make mistakes, Rob. We are only human. When Caitlin became ill Sarah and I went through a rough patch. I found it hard to cope with the diagnosis and someone I was working with very closely at the time offered a shoulder to cry on. I fell for her like a pubescent teenager. Just the memory makes me shiver, even now. I was about to lose everything that I really loved when I realised that I had made a mistake, a huge, massive, stupid mistake," Fletcher says, his head bowed. "And did you tell your wife?" I ask. "Yes, that was the toughest thing. I did not want her to find out from anyone else. Frankly, I believe the entire hospital knew about it but Sarah didn't have a clue. She was devastated. Her daughter had suffered kidney failure and her husband was sleeping with a theatre nurse – not great...," As Fletcher pauses I am thinking of Angie and then Beth. My eyes are scanning the busy pub. We are the only men with children here. Strangers may think that we are a gay couple, all huddled up at the table, having an intimate conversation. "I don't believe Angie will ever forgive me," I say sadly. "No, Rob. You can't expect that. Would you if she cheated on you? But you can make it work if you are honest with each other. I had to sit down and explain myself – and if that was not difficult enough I had to continue working with that nurse and watch her seduce another surgeon. It made my life hell until we managed to shift her to another department." Fletcher takes a deep breath. His ability to stay totally in control of his emotions is unbelievable. He appears so composed. "If I tried to explain myself to Angie she would never understand. I don't understand it myself. I don't believe there is any chance at all," I say. "I bet there is, Rob – provided you really, really want her back," Fletcher disagrees.

As we leave the pub I feel strangely rejuvenated. We had come here to have a meal and discuss Fletcher's shocking discovery but we ended up trying to solve my marital problems.

Once I have put Jordan and Melanie to bed Fletcher invites me for one final beer in the lounge. "Go on, Rob. Tell me about that affair of yours," he encourages me - and so I talk until the early hours of the morning.

The children and I leave Fletcher and the cottage after lunch early on Sunday afternoon. My cousin's flight home is booked for the following Thursday morning which means that he will have to leave Crantock on Wednesday. "I'll ring you as soon as I've spoken to my doctor," I promise as we say our good-byes. Jordan hugs his newly-found uncle. "I want to visit you in Australia next year," he says, the tone of his voice full of excitement. "Yes, of course. You can all come to visit. We have a big house," Fletcher replies. Then he puts his large hand onto my shoulder. "Thank you for everything you've done for me, Rob. I think, I will leave sleeping dogs lie and not pursue my paternal roots any further – not for now, at least, but I'll let you know what happens with my mother's will when I get any news," he says. I still feel uncomfortable about that but I resist any comment. "We'll keep in touch," I respond firmly. The thought of losing the cottage still concerns me deeply but I know that the property is not the most pressing issue for my cousin at the moment.

As I drive the children back to their mother I recall Fletcher's words. "...provided you really, really want her back..." Do I really want Angie back? Do I want Beth? Now that her calls and texts have stopped is she perhaps on to the next lover? I don't know what to think anymore.

Jordan, in the back seat of my car, is totally wound up. He asks me how much it will cost to fly to Australia, how long the flight will be, what the weather will be like and if we can go swimming every day when we get there. Melanie has gone to sleep next to him in the baby seat. "Look, Jordan, before we discuss this any further we will need to talk to Mum about Uncle Fletcher," I tell my son. What I don't say to him is that I will need to speak to Angie urgently should my initial blood test results reveal that I could be a potential donor. Apart from Fletcher and the staff at my new doctor's surgery no one knows that I am considering becoming a donor. Perhaps I should start by asking Angie if she is prepared to have a serious conversation with me during the next couple of days.

When we arrive at my former home Angie is pleased to see me – not that she has changed her mind about the divorce but her vacuum cleaner is broken and after taking it apart into several piece she is struggling to fit them together again. I can hear her curse as we approach the front door. "Hi," she greets us, wiping the dust off her face, "Rob, do you think you could have a look at that Hoover please?" With that she hands me a number of dirty grey plastic parts that have come off the appliance. "Of course, let's have a look," I agree happily.

While I am occupied with the vacuum cleaner Jordan tells his mother about Fletcher. I am by far too busy to listen to the conversation that is taking place in the lounge. It is not until Angie offers me a cup of tea that she says: "What's all this about a new uncle, Rob?" I push the Hoover parts further along the kitchen table. "We have recently found out that my aunt Delia has a son," I explain. I am surprised that Angie pulls a chair next to the one I am currently occupying. She seems prepared to listen. So I tell her my version of meeting Fletcher. "So this guy is going to contest his mother's will. He wants the cottage, obviously," Angie remarks angrily. I shrug my shoulders. The children are still playing in the lounge and I resolve to take this opportunity for an important discussion. "Ange, I need to talk to you about a health matter – I've had a blood test and...," I start. Within seconds Angie's face drops. "Oh, dear, Robby. What's up? Are you ill?" she asks, sounding most concerned. It is a very long time ago since she has called me "Robby". "No, I am not. Well, I hope not anyway. I am considering becoming a living organ donor, " I say slowly. "Living?" Angie asks. She wraps her hands around her mug

210

as if to warm them. "Yes, Angie. Fletcher's daughter in Australia needs a kidney, urgently, and if I can help..," My wife won't let me finish. "You want to give up a vital organ and that guy is going to take your property away? Are you completely off your rocker, Rob?" she shouts. "Listen, please calm down, Angie. I don't even know if I am a suitable candidate yet. How would you feel if your child was dying, your only child. Wouldn't you try to find a donor? If a person is fit and healthy they can live with one kidney, Ange. Some people, like Fletcher, are born with just one which is unfortunate and means that he can't be considered for a donation, and his wife has a rare blood disorder, she can't either and....," I am trying to explain. "So if something happens to my kidneys or those of our children and you have already given one kidney away you wouldn't be able to help us," Angie concludes. I pause for a minute. Then I nod. "That's why I want to discuss it with you, Ange. I realise that I am making a huge sacrifice should I be a good match," I say carefully. "You can't expect me to agree, Rob but I suppose at the end of the day it is your decision, your body, your risk. My opinion does not count for anything," Angie says sadly. "It matters to me, Ange. You matter to me," I reply slowly. Angie shakes her head. She pushes the plastic bits back in front of me. "If you can't fix this, Rob, don't worry, I'll ask Charles," she says and leaves the kitchen.

Well, I have certainly messed this one up. If Fletcher thinks I can ever win my wife back then he is mistaken. Perhaps I don't really want her back enough. When the cracks in our marriage started to show maybe it was time to call it a day. I am not sure what to believe anymore. Feeling frustrated and helpless I return to my task of fixing the vacuum cleaner. I can't concentrate, I've lost my nerve.

First thing on Monday morning I make my way to my new GP. I have rarely felt this nervous going to the doctor before. My palms are sweaty and I feel a little sick as I enter the waiting room. Fortunately I don't have to wait long until I am called to the consulting room. My allocated doctor is a middle-aged lady - slim, with short grey hair and lively brown eyes. The smile on her face tells me immediately that she has good news. One hand rooting through papers on her desk and the other typing on her keyboard she turns to me. "All your initial tests have come back fine, Mr Cunningham. You are of a suitable blood type, your renal function is good – all results are normal," she tells me happily. She can see that I am less enthusiastic than she is. Instantly she stops typing. "Should you consider going for the next step, Mr Cunningham, you will be making a very serious decision. I am sure you understand that," my doctor continues. During the next ten minutes she tells me all that Fletcher has already told me, including that, considering the urgency, I should have any further tests done in Australia. The doctor hands me a couple of computer print-outs and leaflets and basically sends me away. Although I have been given a clean bill of health I feel as if I have just received a death sentence. It's decision time, Robert Cunningham!

Slowly I wander back to my car, drop into the driver's seat and ring Fletcher. "It's good news," I say as he answers his mobile and then I burst into tears. My cousin allows me a few seconds to compose myself. After a while he says: "That's great, really great, Rob. I know you will have to work today but please take some time to think about this information. I am still in Crantock, until early Wednesday morning. We can talk tomorrow if you like. The last thing I want is pressurise you."

It takes me another fifteen minutes of shedding tears before I can leave the surgery's car park and drive to work. Red-faced, shaking and generally looking a complete mess, I enter the showroom. Hardly acknowledging my colleagues I proceed to the Managing Director's office. "I'd like to book a couple of days off, please," I tell Harry. Before I can leave his office again he asks me to take a seat. "Will and Theo are concerned about you, Rob. It appears that you are not coping well. We are aware that you are divorcing, and I am sorry to hear that. However, we have a business to run here. We need someone we can rely on, someone who is willing to work, who puts the hours in, over and above what is usually expected. Our remuneration for the post reflects this. We offer great conditions to our staff. If you feel you can't cope with your new position...,"

I don't listen anymore. I don't want to hear it and I certainly don't wish to discuss it. Furiously I get up and leave. I run straight back to the car, jump in and drive off.

Within minutes I have recovered from my rage. Taking a deep breath I tell myself that the job was not right for me from the start. I am still in the probation period which means that I have not signed a contract of employment yet. There is no need for me to work here. I can move away, find another position or even return to golf. With a bit of practice I should be able to play well enough again to qualify for PGA training and become a teaching professional. I don't need to drive this fancy Mercedes – a modest second-hand car will suffice.

With a smile on my face I park my car at the Country Club. My first task will be to give Harry notice for both my position at the dealership and his luxury holiday apartment. I don't need them anymore. If I am not working in Plymouth any longer I can live in Crantock for a while. No, I am not prepared to run away from my problems. I am going to face them head on – and solve them.

It is around 4pm when my mobile rings. I am still sitting on the sofa, my laptop on my knees, researching more kidney donor sites. Reluctantly I look at the phone, hoping it is not the dealership that is ringing. "Fletcher" it reads on the brightly lit screen. Hesitantly I take the call. "Rob, someone has pushed a letter through the door. It is an envelope addressed to you," my cousin reports. "Ok, thanks, I'll look at it tomorrow," I reply casually. "I've taken the day off and I will come and see you on your last day in Cornwall," I continue but Fletcher is still concerned about my mail. "I have been here all afternoon. Nobody knocked or rang the bell. It seems to me that this envelope was forced through the gap under the door in a hurry. It is badly torn und something has dropped out, something like a coin – hang on..." I can hear Fletcher walking around the cottage, the sound of the creaking floor boards a familiar noise to me by now. "It is a ball-marker, I believe, for golf." My heart sinks. It must be my ball-marker, the one I gave to Beth. "Beth! It's from Beth!" I shout out. Suddenly I don't feel so relaxed anymore. Why is she returning it? Why is she in Crantock? "Open the envelope, please, Fletch. Just read the letter out to me," I demand quickly. I can't explain why I am feeling so nervous. Panic is setting in. "Mar not my face but let me be, secure...," Fletcher reads slowly but I interrupt. "What else,

214

Fletch? What else?" I ask desperately. "Nothing else, just that poem or whatever it is," replies my cousin calmly. "It's from Beth, I am sure of it. The words are from a carving in a cave. It's a lethal place at high tide...- I can't go into it all right now but I fear that Beth could be going to that cave and she could well be in danger. Please do me a favour, Fletch, please. You must help me. You must try and find her. When did the envelope arrive? Beth may have gone to the beach, to that cave. Get your trainers on and run, run as fast as you can, along Crantock beach, all the way, to the very end. Run towards West Pentire, the other side of the beach, where I took you for lunch. Just before you get to the steps that lead up from the beach to the coastal path there is a cave, a special one, with the carvings of those words. You'll find it. There is no time. If the tide is in we are in trouble. You must try, please, Fletch. Take your phone with you and shout for Beth. You can't miss her. She is small with short dark hair. If you can't find her anywhere along that beach, ring 999. I cannot ignore this message. It doesn't sound good to me. Go, Fletch, go. I'll come to Crantock as fast as I can," I shout desperately. Although I have not known Beth for very long I know what her message means. I have no doubt that she is down there, down by that cave. She was fascinated by it. If she was going to do something stupid she would go down there... My heart is beating like a drum. I feel physically sick. Trying not to lose my nerve I grab my duvet, a warm jacket and a bottle of mineral water. Then I pick up my car keys and run to the car park.

All I can do is drive, without breaking the speed limit too often, thinking about Fletcher and hoping that he will find Beth. It is getting dark, and my cousin does not know the area well. He will be on his own unless there is someone local on the beach, a dog walker perhaps, someone who may have seen Beth. I am so worried, so confused that I am in danger of causing an accident. Like a maniac I drive my company Mercedes along country roads, overtaking where I normally wouldn't, risk it all, just to get to Crantock. I can only wonder how Fletcher is getting on. Shaking like to leaf I am trying to convince myself that my cousin is fast, a born athlete, a very strong, fantastic runner – and that he is a doctor, well qualified to deal with emergencies. He will catch up with her. I know he will...

The thought of Beth drowning in that horribly cold sea, Beth the brilliant swimmer who loves Crantock so much! Should I ring 999 before Fletcher gets to the cave, alert the coastguard? What if it was just a scam, just a devious attempt to get me to contact her? I may be wrong. Maybe it is Beth's way of ending our relationship but why those words, why nothing else? Beth is capable of all kind of things. She has such vivid imagination! The characters in her books, her stories – they would do something drastic like this. Why would she deliver the letter to the cottage on a day when she must assume that I am in Plymouth? She cannot possibly know that Fletcher is staying there. Why is she doing this to me? Will Fletcher ring me if he finds her? As I drive along my mobile remains silent. I am aware that Fletcher could well be in a dangerous situation himself while trying to rescue her.

I cannot wait to get to the scene. As I approach Crantock heavy mist has turned into fog, wet veils drifting across the fields near the entrance to the village. With the windscreen wipers of my Mercedes working at full speed I debate where to park the car. I am too anxious to think clearly. Where is the best place to approach the cave by car? Should I go through the village, take the narrow road that leads to the coast path, abandon the car and run to the beach? I've never tried to find the cave from the top of the cliffs. The sky is completely dark now and visibility poor. I decide to drive towards West Pentire, trying to assess the state of the tide when the phone rings. Knowing very well that it is illegal to use a mobile phone while driving I take the risk and answer the call. "Where are you, Rob? No need to panic. I've got her. All is well," Fletcher reports. I cannot describe how relieved I am. I cannot thank Fletcher enough. "We'll meet you at the car park," he says calmly but I can hear that he is breathing heavily, gasping for air as he speaks. His voice sounds low and hoarse. "Ok, I... - I..ok - see you there...," I stutter nervously. Heaving a sigh of relief I turn the Mercedes around and drive straight to Crantock Village. Speeding through the village centre and down the beach road I reach the lower car park. I make no attempt to park properly. I simply drive as close to the high dune as I can and then I jump out of the car, run through the deep sand, scramble up the dune to the point where Brian Henderson stood on that fateful evening. Below, on the beach, in the fine drizzle, I spot two people walking along, one very tall, one very small – there is no doubt about it, it's Fletcher and Beth. They walk fast, and it does not appear that they are talking. As they come closer I can clearly see that Fletcher's wild hair is wet, dripping onto his neck and shoulders. My cousin looks like he has been in a washing machine, his soaked clothes sticking to his large body. Beth is wrapped in an over-sized jacket, which is no doubt Fletcher's. My heart is missing a beat and I just run, run down the dune towards the beach until I reach them. I have never seen human beings shake as much as Beth and my cousin do. Both look desperately cold. Although I feel like saying something no words come over my lips. I am in shock. "Close call," I hear Fletcher say through chattering teeth. I look at Beth but I don't feel like hugging her.

In silence we all climb back up the dune and down again to where I have left my Mercedes. I rush to get the duvet out of the boot and put it around Beth. Fletcher, still shaking violently, helps me push my freezing mistress into the passenger seat. "You go on, I'll jog back," he insists. I nod and jump into the driver's seat. Within seconds I drive off. My cousin has already reached the road.

Beth is by far too cold to speak. She sits in the passenger seat shivering. I have so many questions on my mind but I am too nervous to ask any. In front of the cottage I do all I can to get her out of the car quickly and upstairs under the warm shower. Before I feel ready to say anything to Beth Fletcher has also arrived. I help Beth up the stairs but I refuse assisting her to get undressed. Leaving her in the bathroom I make my way down the stairs. My cousin, coughing and trying to clear his throat, has already started stripping off by the front door. I rush back up to the single room to fetch another duvet. Not being equipped with central heating the cottage does not offer much warmth. Dropping a heap of wet and sandy clothes my cousin covers himself up gratefully. "I'll get the fire going again," I say, searching for a lighter and some old newspapers. Fletcher follows me to the lounge and sinks into the ancient armchair. Still breathing heavily he watches me work. I am no expert at lighting fires but after a couple of failed attempts I manage to keep a flame alive.

When Beth comes down into the lounge, wrapped in a large bath towel, we realise that she has no dry clothes to put on. Fletcher sends me upstairs to his suitcase to select some of his clothes as a temporary measure. As I dig deep into his half-packed case I find the photograph and the newspaper cutting of Colin Fletcher among the garments. Carefully I push them to the bottom and then I pull out a clean t-shirt which will be like a dress on Beth. Trying not to disturb the suitcase any further I grab Fletcher's cardigan that is lying on his bed. Last I pick up a worn pair of running socks which have been left under the dressing table and return to the lounge. Both Beth and my cousin are sitting on the floor in front of the fire now, one wrapped in a single duvet, the other in a long towel. Although the flames are raging both are still shivering. Silently I pass Beth Fletcher's clothes. "Here, put these on," I say. I should be feeling sorry for her but I do not. "I will go and take my shower," Fletcher decides and gets up. I am glad that he leaves us alone for a few minutes. As soon as he is out of sight Beth drops her towel in front of me. "You've seen me naked before," she whispers seductively as she changes into Fletcher's enormous t-shirt. Determined to ignore her remark I turn away and offer to make tea. While I am in the kitchen I suddenly realise that I still have no desire to even hug Beth. It seems that all my love for her has disappeared. Everything inside me has somehow frozen. I feel nothing - no lust, no love, not even kindness. My heart is running on empty but my head feels light and clear. I put the kettle on. This is the end of our affair.

Once Fletcher returns all three of us congregate around the blazing fire. Fortunately Beth and my cousin have stopped shaking. They are sipping their teas when I ask: "So tell me, what actually happened?" Fletcher, fresh, fully dressed, his long fingers combing the shiny blond curls out of his face, is looking at Beth, waiting for her to answer but she has her head bowed and says nothing. "To put it all into a nutshell – you almost lost both of us this afternoon," he replies sadly. I look from one to the other. "Why did you do that, Beth? If Fletcher had not rung me when he found your envelope and if I had not sent him out to find you, you would have died. Is that what you wanted? Why?" I ask angrily. Instantly Fletcher raises his hand, signalling for me to calm down but I do not take the hint. This time it is I who paces up and down the lounge in the same way as Fletcher had done over the last few days. "Because....," Beth whimpers but she cannot continue. Tears are streaming down her face. She looks at me helplessly. "I'll leave you two for a moment. And please, Rob, be gentle," Fletcher says kindly and walks out of the room. As so many times in recent days I am grateful to him. I wait until he has closed the door behind himself. Then I shake my head. "Because what, Beth? Because you are attention-seeking and selfish, because you want me to feel guilty for the rest of my life, because you want to bully me into loving you, living with you – but I tell you what – I have realised that that is not what I want, not anymore. I have learned that there are more important aspects to life than earning lots of money, driving a fancy car and having an affair. It's not about you, Beth. I've lost all respect for myself over the last few months but I am determined to change. I'm going to make a real difference to someone's life. I will be going to Australia where I will hopefully be able to donate one of my kidneys to Fletcher's sick daughter. I have given up my new job in Plymouth and I am going to live here for a while – on my own – and maybe, just maybe, I will one day be able to return to my wife and family. I am sorry. I wish our relationship did not have to end this way." Sighing I walk around the coffee table. I spot the ball-marker, pick it up and put it in my pocket. "And I will return your ring," I say firmly. There is a moment of silence before Beth responds: "If you don't want to give it your own daughter why don't you give it to Fletcher's daughter. She may appreciate it...," she whispers softly. Then she attempts to dry her eyes with the sleeve of Fletcher's high quality cardigan. "I had no idea that you have an Australian cousin. That man has been a hero today," she continues.

I do not respond but leave the lounge to look for Fletcher. He is upstairs. A monotonous and dull noise around the cottage tells me that he must have put the wet clothes in the washing machine, and right now I watch him changing the bed linen in the single room. "I don't want her to stay the night, Fletch," I say strictly. Again combing his golden hair out of his face he stops working. "You don't have much choice, Rob. Beth's clothes won't be dry until tomorrow and we will need to keep an eye on her to ensure that she is safe," he explains. His blue eyes go through me while the tone of his voice sounds very serious. I dare not argue with him.

Later that evening we order a rather expensive take-away - and have it delivered to the door. The atmosphere in the cottage feels rather tense. I would have loved to have a couple of beers with my food but Fletcher's advice is to give alcohol a miss. Although I have still not been told the whole story of the dramatic rescue I know that my cousin is concerned about Beth's mental health.

I am tempted to make my excuses and drive back to Saltash, leaving Fletcher with Beth, but I decide last minute that it would hardly be fair. Somehow I am hoping that Beth, being by far the lightest and smallest of us, will offer to sleep in the lounge but needless to say it falls to me to spend the night on a much too short, creaky, worn-out and uncomfortable sofa. I get little sleep. Checking the time on my mobile phone almost every hour I simply cannot rest. Apart from my discomfort too many questions occupy my mind. It is 6am when I realise that Fletcher is pottering around in the kitchen. Determined to hear his account of yesterday's events I get up from the sofa. Taking care not to disturb the floor boards I creep towards the kitchen. From the door I observe my cousin folding a pile of freshly washed clothes. He is in his running kit, the wild curls tamed into a pony-tail. "Good morning," I greet him slowly. One glace at the kitchen window tells me that it is still dark outside and it is raining. "Surely you are not going to run in this weather?" I ask while putting the kettle on. "I need to get out, Rob, get some fresh air," he replies. I instantly detect that sadness in his voice, that small trace of melancholy. "Of course, just don't expect me to join you today," I respond with a wry smile. "No, you will have to stay here and look after Beth. She cannot be left alone," he says, and with that he hands me the dry washing.

Once again I feel a little inadequate in his presence. He does not smile as he pushes past me and leaves the cottage.

"Yes, boss!" I whisper. As I turn around I realise that Beth has been watching us. Smiling she joins me in the kitchen. "Good morning," she greets me. It is just her and me now but there is no spark in my body. How can this attractive woman who has given me the most exciting sex of my life suddenly mean nothing to me? I glaze at her. "Tea?" I ask her quickly while filling the kettle with fresh water. "Thank you," she responds softly. I sense that she wants to touch me, maybe even kiss me. Instinctively I step away from her. Apart from the rain drumming onto the small cottage windows it is very quiet in the kitchen. "Your cousin is amazing, Rob, truly amazing," Beth enthuses. I remain stone-faced. "Ok, so why don't you tell me what happened yesterday," I ask as I pull a couple of mugs out of the cupboard. Beth is fighting tears again. This time I am determined not to let her off the hook. A week ago I would have taken her into my arms, I would have hugged and kissed her but now I just stand and watch her suffering. "I wanted to die," she whispers slowly as she follows me into the lounge. Covering her face with both hands she drops into one of the old armchairs opposite my churned up emergency bed. She is still dressed in nothing but Fletcher's large t-shirt, looking small and pale, her hair untidy. "I drove to Newquay and parked the car," she starts. I can see that she is freezing but I resist offering her the sofa or my blanket. Instead I begin to arrange fresh logs in the fire place. "I am listening," I say, turning my back to her. "I took the public bus to come here and I deliberately chose a day when I expected you to be at work, thinking that the cottage would be empty," she explains. "I pushed the envelope under the door and walked towards the coast path." Although I manage to get the fire going swiftly I dare not turn around while Beth is talking. "I climbed down onto the beach, walked towards the cave with the carvings. The tide was already quite far in but I wanted to get there before the water could reach it. I sat down on a slippery flat rock, got my bottle out and a packet of strong painkillers. It was then that I heard someone call my name. I could not believe how rapidly the water was rising around my rock. I must have put the pills down for a second to look who was shouting and the tide took them away, just like that – gone...That's when I panicked. I could see someone running through the water towards me. I wanted to shout for help but the power of the waves had pulled me off the rock, straight into the water. It was already pretty deep at that point. I stayed afloat and waved. Luckily Fletcher spotted me. He had to swim, fight the rip currents but somehow managed to grab me. The water must have been up to my neck, at least, but I can't remember. It all happened so fast. Fletcher carried me the last bit, through the deep, cold water onto the beach. He told me that he is a lifeguard and all would be fine..." As Beth takes a break from recalling her ordeal I turn around. "A lifeguard!" I comment slowly. "Yes, that's what he said. He checked me over and gave me his jacket. Once I had recovered a little he called you. Then we started walking and he told me that he is your cousin from Australia and that he is staying at the cottage, that he found my letter and rang you. I can't remember anymore than that. I was too cold to talk and I felt awful." I am about to make another comment when we hear the key being turned in the front door. Fletcher has returned, so I get up to speak to him. "It's time we had some breakfast," I decide and make my way back to the kitchen.

Minutes later I can hear Fletcher talking to Beth at the bottom of the staircase. It appears that they are arguing over who will use the shower first. I am yawning. The fact that I have effectively lost my job yesterday has not bothered me much until now. For some reason I feel guilty. I realise that I should take the car back this afternoon. If I am not returning to my office I will no longer have a right to a swish company car.

It is good to see Beth dressed in her own clothes again. She is tucking into her breakfast and she seems generally more relaxed. "I have told Rob about the rescue while you were out," she tells Fletcher proudly. "That's good. I'm glad you felt able to do that. You should try and get some help, Beth – professional help, I mean," my cousin suggests. His words sound kind, fatherly. Beth shakes her head. "I don't think I will need that now. I know it was silly. I promise you I won't try anything like that ever again," she replies smiling confidently. "That is the standard response, Beth – and unfortunately a high percentage of patients will try again – and succeed," Fletcher says. Beth keeps smiling sexily at my cousin. "You sounded like a doctor then, Fletch," she chuckles. "I am. Not that psychiatry was my favourite subject at Med School but...," he responds calmly. Beth is frowns. "Oh, I am sorry, I thought you were a lifeguard," she says apologetically. "Yes, that too. Well, I qualified as a lifeguard when I was a student but haven't had time to spend hours on the beach since," Fletcher admits. He takes a deep breath and adds: "So, I do know what I am talking about, Beth. It is not just a matter of getting back into your car and driving home." While Beth is digesting this news I wonder how I can help. It is Fletcher's last day in the UK, and I know he is desperate to get back to his wife and daughter.

Before we get into any further discussions about Beth's future I receive the not unexpected call from the dealership. Harry, the Managing Director, has read my letter of resignation and the notice for his luxury apartment at the Country Club. He is actually apologising for not letting me have a couple of days off, and he is trying to persuade me to return to work next week. "I am sorry," I tell him in no uncertain terms, "but I have made my decision. I will leave my position with immediate effect and I will stand by my notice for the flat. Later on this afternoon I will be returning the car and clear out my office." Although I am many miles away, in my mind's eye I can see young Theo jumping for joy and Will rubbing his hands with glee. I am sure both will be pleased to see me leave for good.

Due to the heavy rain outside and the lounge being the best place for successful mobile phone reception both Beth and Fletcher are forced to listen to the conversation. "Done it!" I report proudly while turning my mobile off. My cousin looks most concerned. "You haven't just packed your job in, have you?" he asks me. "Yes, I have. I'll take some time out and come to Australia for further tests. I shall look for new employment in the UK when I return," I say decisively. "I can see your wife balking at that," Fletcher remarks cautiously. "Yes, maybe, but like she said – it is my life, my body and ultimately my decision. I may have to dig into our savings to support my family for a while but once I get the cottage in order I may be able to let it again while I am away – unless your lawyers throw a spanner into the works, of course!" I respond. Fletcher leaves the creaking armchair and begins to pace around the room like he always does when things get difficult. "They won't. I won't let them," he confirms.

Deep inside I am celebrating a small victory over my cousin but at the same time I realise that I may be paying a huge price in return.

All the logs in the fire place have burnt down. It is already beginning to feel chilly in the lounge. Beth who has been very quiet during the last quarter of an hour rushes to rekindle the dying flame. "I was hoping to buy this cottage for myself," she says while dealing with the firewood. "I have asked my literary agent to purchase it on my behalf so you wouldn't know that I am the buyer. We did not expect you to withdraw the cottage from the market," she says to me. "My life was suddenly in such disarray that I did not want to carry on. Brian and his legal team were trying their utmost to make our separation difficult for me. Our sons were constantly begging me to give you up. You never answered any of my calls, the place that I was hoping would offer me some kind of respite and sanctuary was suddenly no longer available. I just did not know what to do anymore. I had no one to talk to so I made the decision to end it all before it would drive me crazy," she explains. She has managed to restore warmth for us but I am shivering now. Her words make me feel guilty. As she returns to her seat I can see her tears. I realise that I should say sorry, perhaps take her into my arms but I cannot do it.

Fletcher has his hands folded behind his head, subconsciously taming his unruly hair. "That's what I mean. You need to talk to someone about your situation. You should not have to deal with all this on your own," he says calmly. Turning my head our eyes meet. When I think about what he has to deal with I cannot help admiring him.

"Maybe you are right but first of all I need to go home," Beth mutters under her breath. "I can take you back to your car when I take mine back to Plymouth after lunch," I offer immediately. Fletcher raises his hands to stop me. "No, hang on, under no circumstances will I allow Beth to drive," he decides. A hint of a smile appears on my ex-lover's sad face. "I got rid of the car keys on the beach. They are somewhere in the deep blue sea," she admits. "Good. Ideally you could do with picking up but you could go home by train as long as someone meets you at the station when you arrive," Fletcher replies strictly. Beth nods. "I will ring my sons. Hopefully, they will agree to do that," she answers. "Then let me drive you to Truro railway station," I insist. "Thank you, Rob," Beth replies tenderly. We both know how hard this journey will be for us but at least Fletcher does not disagree this time.

We decide to have an early lunch in the pub. It has stopped raining and the three of us walk down the road in silence. I am sure this is not how Fletcher has imagined his last day in Cornwall.

Saying good-bye to my cousin and wishing him a safe journey is not a big issue. My mind is made up. I will keep in close contact with him which also means that I will probably see him again very soon.

However, getting into my car with Beth is another matter. She has reluctantly made all the arrangements for her arrival in Surrey and she has promised us to look after herself and seek professional help as soon as possible. On the outside Beth appears to be back in control now. She is no longer tearful. No doubt she takes more notice of my cousin than me.

It is I who finds it difficult to cope with the present state of affairs. Nervously I get into the driver's seat of my executive-style car for the last time. I don't know how to act, don't know what to say to Beth but silence is definitely the worst.

We have barely left the village when Beth says: "I know you want nothing to do with me anymore, Rob but should you find that you are not suitable for that organ donation, please ask Fletcher to get in touch with me. I would also be prepared to help if I can." Her words surprise me. I nod and say: "Thank you."

As I drive towards Truro I am feeling very emotional. My pulse is racing. In less than thirty minutes I will finally have to let go and say farewell to Beth. Although I no longer desire her I find it hard to end our relationship.

I have to concentrate on the road but I notice that Beth is looking out of the window with a forlorn expression. Deep down she is suffering too. If only we had never got into this situation. We are both to blame for letting it happen. After another long spell of silence Beth suddenly says: "You are doing the right thing, Rob. I want you to know that. I hope, for everyone concerned, that all this mess we've got ourselves into is the beginning of something positive. You have made a brave decision and it will be rewarded. I honestly believe that." I am not sure that I agree but I resist a comment. "Thank you, Beth," I simply say hoping that her words will be true.

Much too soon we reach Truro station. I park the Mercedes in the short-stay car park and follow Beth to the ticket machine. I use my credit card to pay for her fare. As the seconds to our final good-bye tick on I can feel myself weakening. Instinctively I put my arms around Beth and hug her tightly. "Promise me to look after yourself, promise me to stay away from me, promise...," I whisper. "I've got to go," is all she says and then she slips through the barriers and onto the platform. She does not look back, I do not wave. Slowly I walk back to my car. "Plymouth next," I say to the vehicle, quickly patting its shiny bonnet.

Handing the car back and picking up my few belongings from the office is less stressful than seeing Beth off. Once I am on the bus back to the apartment in Saltash I feel free. I am glad to be back in my temporary home but before I start packing up I ring Justin. I have not spoken to him for a while and I want him to know what has happened. He will also have to help me sort out some wheels. I will need a car if I am going to live in Crantock.

Have I once said that my wife can talk to her best friend Barbara for hours? Well, today I am beating all the records with my long conversation with Justin. He cannot quite believe my story but I assure him that it is all fact.

Within a couple of days I am the proud owner of an old rusty and unreliable-looking Landrover that has been waiting at Justin's garage for the scrap merchant. It still has a few months MOT left and has cost me next to nothing to buy. Justin has named it "Hetty". I am not planning on keeping her long but she has managed to move all my personal belongings from Saltash to Crantock in one safe trip so I am satisfied.

So, this is the beginning of my new life – I am unattached and unemployed, drive an ancient banger, live in an old cottage without double glazing and central heating and I am as happy as I have been for many years. I have also decided to grow a beard. Not losing sight of the possibility of a forthcoming operation I go running every day, even in the rain, and keep myself as fit and healthy as I can.

On the Friday before my next "father's weekend" I ring Angie and plead with her to let me visit for a serious discussion about the future. As expected she is reluctant but I have rehearsed my words for so long that I am prepared for any onslaught of criticism. I stay calm and finally get what I want. "OK. Why don't you come over straight after work," Angie offers kindly. "I am not working today," I reply truthfully. "In that case it may be best for you to come here when Jordan is still at school," Angie replies. "Fine. I'll be with you at 12.30pm," I say quickly. "You may as well come for lunch – I've got some food left over from last night," Angie offers. Her invitation surprises me but I accept gratefully. "Thank you. That's great. Is there anything you want me to bring – for dessert maybe?" I ask immediately. "Up to you. See you later," Angie replies.

I do my utmost to make our lunch a memorable one. I buy flowers, wine and chocolates for Angie, treats for the kids and a large bowl of the supermarket's finest trifle for after lunch. I even dress up a little. It is strange but it feels to me like going on a first date. Although I have prepared myself meticulously I am terribly nervous as I drive towards Launceston. As I turn into "our" road the butterflies are gathering for a mass invasion in my stomach.

I park the old Diesel at the top of the drive and straighten my tie. Nervously I walk around the Landrover to retrieve the huge bouquet of flowers and the gifts from the passenger seat. Fully laden I approach the front door. Luckily Angie must have heard me slam the tinny car doors. As she opens the door I step backwards. I almost fall over. Seriously, I hardly recognise my wife. Her straw blond hair has been cut very short and the colour has changed to a shiny chestnut tone. "Wow, Ange – I love your new hairstyle!" I comment instantly. She takes a little twirl in the porch and smiles until she spots the Landrover. "Whose is that?" she asks pointing at the greenish-brown rust-bucket. "That's Hetty. She's mine," I reply, trying to sound proud. "What's happened to the Mercedes?" Angie asks as she takes the flowers off me. "Gone back. All will be revealed!" I respond secretively. The expression on Angie's face looks less than impressed.

I enter what I still call "our" kitchen and notice that Angie has laid up for us – not like she normally does for a family meal but for two, using our special crockery. The table looks lovely, arranged for an important visitor, a valued guest. I watch Angie put the flowers into a vase. "You look great, Ange," I say admiringly. Suddenly fear sets in, doubts and a terrible thought – what if Angie has a new man, a boyfriend? What if she has done this because she wants to tell me? All the best-made plans go out of the window in a jiffy. I can neither help nor contain myself. "Are you seeing someone?" I ask straight out. Angie smiles. She can see that I am upset, more than that, furious. "It wouldn't be a problem if I did, would it, Rob?" she responds very calmly. I must admit this scenario has not seriously entered my mind up to now. "Please, take a seat. Would you like a drink?" she asks me formally. I am thinking of a whole bottle of whisky, anything to kill this horrible feeling of jealousy that is building up in my gut but I reply: "Just a cup of tea would be lovely, Ange. I am driving." Angie puts the kettle on. It is surprisingly quiet in the house and I am wondering where my daughter is. "Where is Melanie?" I ask. "She is next door for an hour or so," Angie explains.

My suspicion that Angie has to tell me something very important is increasing by the minute. I don't feel good. It begins to dawn on me that Angie is taking my request for a private conversation as an opportunity to advise me of her new partner. My wife checks the timer on the oven. Then she turns around and says: "I have been thinking about what you told me the last time you were here and I believe that I was wrong to have such a go at you. You have made a very brave and remarkable decision. If your kidney really is a good match for your cousin's daughter and if you are able to save that girl's life then I will support you." "Support me?" I repeat lamely. I can feel the heat rising into my cheeks, my heart pumping fast. Something is not right here.

"Yes, support you, Rob. I will not stand in your way or make it difficult for you. What more do you expect?" she asks. The realisation that I have to be honest from now on makes me feel even more uneasy. I bow my head, then lift it again and come clean: "As it is urgent for Caitlin I will have to go to Australia for more tests. I may be away for some time and I have therefore decided to give up work for a while." Now that the words are out I try to control my breathing. Angie is visibly stunned. "You have what? Given up work? Who is going to pay the mortgage, pay for the children? What on earth has happened to you, Rob? You can't just run away from your responsibilities! And there is a chance that you may lose the cottage!" Angie is outraged. Her well made-up face has lost all expression, all colour.

"It is going to be fine, Ange. I am unlikely to lose the cottage and I will meet all my responsibilities while I am away. I have done my sums. You were right from the start. I did not enjoy working in Plymouth. Please don't think that I am making excuses but perhaps I am – I was hoping that the new job would mean a new start for me when our marriage started to crumble. Then I got involved with Beth Henderson but that is behind me now. That chapter of my life is over – and looking back I am not proud of it," I say humbly. To my utmost surprise Angie takes my hand. Her fingers are softly rubbing the by now barely visible white tan line caused by the removal of my wedding ring. She is fighting to regain her composure before serving our meal. Sitting opposite me she assesses my face quietly. I sense that she is not sure about the new grey stubble. There is a long pause before she speaks. "You know, Robby," she starts slowly, "I really thought I was done with you. After what you've done to me, to us, I thought I would not miss you. I thought I didn't love you anymore and then I met Andy. He is a widower, a single dad and really, really lovely but every time we met for a coffee or went to the cinema it felt wrong. I was wishing I could be with you, and I realised that our friendship would never be more than that, Robby. I didn't tell Jordan about Andy. There was nothing to say about two lonely people spending a little time together. I can't speak for Andy but I don't want it to go any further. If it is not too late I'd rather be with an unemployed low-life who drives a clapped out Landrover and donates body parts to someone he has never met."

THE END

ABOUT THE AUTHOR

Birte Hosken was born in Germany in 1965. Having met her future husband during an exchange visit to Penzance she moved to Cornwall in 1989. Her fascination with the beauty and mystique of the Cornish coast and countryside has inspired her to take her passion for writing further. Birte has two grown-up children and currently works part-time in the NHS. She is a keen tennis player, enjoys keeping fit, travelling – and, of course, writing. Her first book *Petroc's Church* was published in 2016. *Let Wild Waves Roar* is her second novel.

Printed by Amazon Italia Logistica S.r.l.
Torrazza Piemonte (TO), Italy

11469783R00139